THE BODY ON ARCHANGEL BEACH

An Angela Marchmont Mystery Book 11

CLARA BENSON

MOUNT
STREET
PRESS

ISBN: 978-1-913355-32-6

clarabenson.com

The Body on Archangel Beach

Not-quite-newlywed Angela Marchmont is having a belated honeymoon on the idyllic Greek island of Rhodes, but has barely even unpacked her bathing-suit before an unwelcome encounter with the dead body of a young archaeologist draws her into a tangled web of murder and blackmail.

Everyone thinks Roy Cavell drowned accidentally, but after receiving a cryptic note under her door Angela isn't so sure. Cavell had fallen in love with his employer's beautiful wife Sophia Delisi, leaving a heartbroken fiancée behind him and creating tensions up at the local archaeological dig. Mrs. Delisi is thought to bring bad luck: superstition has it that any man who gets close to her dies. Was Cavell the latest victim of the curse? But then why has someone been searching his luggage? Who is signalling from up at the acropolis? And why is somebody trying to put Angela out of the way?

When a second body turns up Angela becomes even more determined to find out the truth—despite the additional complications of a rival detective she can't shake off, a would-be blackmailer who knows the secrets of her past life, and a husband she'd trust more if only he didn't keep disappearing in the middle of the night.

Investigating a murder wasn't in Angela's plans, but if she wants to survive her honeymoon she has no choice.

Foreword

It is now more than seven years since I sent Angela Marchmont off to America at the end of *The Shadow at Greystone Chase*. I had intended to say goodbye to her forever, but somehow I could never quite shake her off, so after I ended the series I indulged myself from time to time by putting her in the occasional short story.

It seems I wasn't the only person to miss Angela, though, and to this day I still get emails from readers asking me to bring her back. For that reason, and since the year 2023 marks a nice, round ten years since Angela's first appearance in *The Murder at Sissingham Hall*, I thought a good way to celebrate the anniversary would be to write an addition to the series.

So, by popular demand, here it is: *The Body on Archangel Beach*, the eleventh Angela Marchmont mystery. Set two years after the events of *The Shadow at Greystone Chase*, the story follows Angela as her attempts to have a quiet honeymoon on an idyllic Greek island are foiled spectacularly by an unexpected encounter with the dead body of a young archaeologist.

Readers will notice that the story begins with the release of Edgar Valencourt (now going by the name of Merivale) from a French prison, and that he and Angela are now married. If you have not been following the Freddy Pilkington-Soames Adventures and would like to know how Edgar ended up in gaol, why Angela turned him in, and the circumstances of their marriage, you may like to read *A Case of Robbery on the Riviera*, although it's not a pre-requisite for your enjoyment of this book.

Note on location

Rhodes is a Greek island just off the coast of Turkey which was occupied by the Italians during the period of my story. Its main town is also called Rhodes.

Chapter One

A<small>N</small> <small>UNSEASONABLE</small> <small>DAMP</small> mist descended over the old French prison as the dark gave way to dawn, betokening an inauspicious beginning to the day. The prison had been an abbey once: a grand old building formerly home to men of God, but now a repository for the worst of the worst, men whom society hid away, wanting nothing more to do with them. In the thin grey light two warders, their shoulders hunched against the drizzle, escorted their charge across the yard to the gate, throwing him the occasional curious glance, for he was not like the other prisoners. The other inmates were thugs and robbers and common murderers: they dealt in the currency of noise and violence, guns to the head and knives in the dark. This one was different. He came from a high family—that much was obvious from the way he spoke—but he was also a thief many times over, and had finally been caught and punished for it. It was even rumoured that he had murdered a woman once. He did not seem the type, but since he was not the sort to give

1

anything away about himself, who knew what wickedness lay beneath the surface? The warders had tried to find out more about him, but they did not know how to talk to him, and found themselves inadvertently calling him by the formal *vous* instead of *tu* before the other prisoners, which was not good for discipline, and so at last they had given it up.

He had done terrible things—it must be true, or why would he be here?—but he was not to be treated too harshly, they had been told. The order had come from on high—as high as it was possible to get, the prison governor had intimated with a significant glance. The prisoner would serve his sentence quietly and would not give them any trouble, he said. And it was true: the man had kept to himself, sitting in his cell day after day, writing letters or reading, causing no disturbance, until today, when he was to be released.

They stopped at a room where the prisoners' effects were kept, and handed their charge a small valise and the few articles that he had once kept in his pockets.

'You weren't here long, considering what you did,' said one warder curiously as the prisoner put a cigarette-case into his pocket and counted the small amount of money they had returned to him. 'You must know people in high places.'

The man did not bother to reply.

'I guess you'll miss us,' said the other. The prisoner darted him an ironic glance and the warder sniggered and went to open the gate that led to the outside, and to freedom.

'He'll be back,' he said to his companion as they shut the gate behind him.

Outside the man looked about him. It was early and there was no-one about, not even a horse or a wagon. It was a good six or seven miles to the nearest station. He might have had a motor-car come to pick him up but he preferred not to draw attention to himself, to move around unnoticed. It was a habit he had developed over the years, and he saw no reason to abandon it.

He hoisted up his valise and set off. Twenty yards ahead of him a stationary car was waiting by the side of the road, long and sleek, an unusual sight in the small town. As he looked at it the door opened and a well-dressed woman alighted and turned to face him. He stopped dead. The two of them regarded one another in silence.

'I thought we'd agreed you'd wait for me in New York,' said Edgar.

'I wasn't about to let you run off again,' replied Angela, trying not to smile too broadly.

———

THE CAR WAS A POWERFUL ONE, eating up the miles easily and soon putting a happy distance between them and the prison. The two passengers sat up straight in the back, being very stiff and polite towards one another in the English way. If the driver, a taciturn Frenchman, noticed the slight awkwardness, he made no sign of it.

'Where's this fellow taking us?' Edgar wanted to know.

'Paris first. I thought you might like to get some new things and have a decent meal. Then we sail tomorrow from Cherbourg on the *Olympic*.'

'Is everything still all right at the farm? What about Nightshade?'

'He's very well. Dan has everything in hand, and said to tell you that he thinks Nightshade is a dead cert, or a *shoo-in*, as he calls it, for Kentucky, and perhaps even the Triple Crown.'

'Hmph. He always was a ridiculous optimist,' said Edgar, although he did not seem displeased at the idea. 'You didn't really think I'd run off, did you?' he added after a minute.

'No-o. Or did I? I don't know. I'll admit I had a slight nagging doubt that you might have been keeping with the wrong sort of company, gone native and started hankering after your former life.'

'I can't say I've been tempted particularly, although some of the old lags have some interesting stories to tell. Is that really why you came, instead of waiting at home?' He turned his head to look at her curiously, then his eyebrows lifted. 'Good heavens, I do believe you missed me!'

Angela bridled.

'Nonsense!' She eyed him sideways. 'Well, perhaps just a little.'

They both laughed, and the awkwardness eased a touch.

Edgar said:

'It's a pity we couldn't have had a proper honeymoon, but I really need to see to the horses. Dan's as capable as they come, but I can't leave the place to him forever. You don't mind, do you?'

'Of course not.'

'We'll do it some other time. Perhaps next year. No trouble with the press, I take it?'

'None at all,' replied Angela. 'I thought it might get into all the newspapers, but I haven't had so much as a telephone-call. It seems the reporters have more exciting things to bother their heads about. I rather think we'll be able to live perfectly quietly without any trouble.'

———

THEY WERE JUST FINISHING dinner at the Ritz when a man of about forty-five, sporting a straggly moustache and a little too much hair oil, approached their table in an oblique manner and gave them a smile that disappeared before it could reach his eyes.

'Mr. Edgar Merivale? Or Valencourt, should I say,' he said, in an accent that gave him away as American. 'Penn Piper's the name. I'm with the *New York City Talker*. You don't mind if I join you, do you?'

He pulled out a chair and placed himself in it.

'As a matter of fact, I do,' replied Edgar.

'Oh, that's a pity,' said Penn Piper easily, without getting up. 'It's just I had word from a little bird—say, that rhymes—that two people of interest were to be found here, so I thought I'd scoot along and see what you had to say for yourselves.'

'About what?'

'My sources tell me that you just spent eight months enjoying the hospitality of the French government for killing a man.'

'Your sources are misinformed,' Edgar said coldly, regarding him with some distaste.

Penn Piper waved a hand.

'That's after you confessed to another murder in England and then faked your own death.' His eye fell on Angela and he favoured her with another smile. 'And Mrs. Angela Marchmont. Of course, you're well known in London. Wasn't it the murder of *your* husband Mr. Valencourt confessed to?' He cocked his head and assumed a knowing expression. 'Two people who ought to hate each other sitting as cosy as you like, having dinner together.

Now, isn't that just the strangest coincidence? There's a story here, I said to myself, and I'm the man to tell it.'

'It's not a coincidence, and nobody murdered anybody,' replied Angela, ignoring a warning glance from Edgar.

Mr. Penn Piper adopted what was presumably meant to be a sympathetic, confidential manner.

'Well, then, suppose you tell me what really happened.' He rooted in his pocket and brought out a notebook.

'You can put that thing away,' said Edgar. 'We're not talking to you. And I'd be obliged if you'd leave us alone to finish our dinner.'

'But you've already finished,' pointed out Penn Piper. 'And it's of interest to the public, you might say.'

'We might not say,' said Angela. 'We're not playing, thank you.'

'Shouldn't you like to clear your name?' asked Piper, as Edgar looked around and caught the eye of the maître d'hotel.

'I did clear my name,' replied Angela crossly.

'Not in the court of public opinion. I guess they wouldn't be too happy to find out you two are consorting together. Why, they might even get the impression there was some collusion between you in the matter of your husband's death.'

Edgar stood up and jerked a thumb towards the door.

'Get out, before I lose my temper and throw you out.'

The maître d'hotel, a purposeful glint in his eye, was bearing down upon them. Penn Piper rose unhurriedly and prepared to retreat.

'I'll be seeing you again,' he said amiably, and strolled out.

Angela was pink in the face.

'*Beastly* press! Oh dear, this is all my fault!'

'Don't be ridiculous,' snapped Edgar, sitting down again. 'How could it possibly be your fault?'

It was not exactly a good start to a marriage to be constantly demanding reassurance, so Angela swallowed her guilt and did not pursue the matter. They had sent the reporter away with a flea in his ear, and she comforted herself with the thought that there was no reason to suppose he would give them any more trouble. Presumably Piper was stationed in Paris permanently for his magazine, and they were leaving for Cherbourg the next day so would not see him again.

The next morning was full of bustle, but at last they departed from the hotel in a taxi and arrived at the station for the next stage of their journey. The porter was instructed as to the disposition of their luggage, and they settled themselves into a first-class carriage.

'On the way at last!' said Edgar. 'I must say, I'll be glad to get home.'

He seemed happier than he had the day before, already beginning to throw off the prison gloom. Angela returned his smile, but her relief was not to last long.

'Well, hallo,' came a familiar voice from the doorway. They looked up and Angela's heart sank. It was the persistent Mr. Penn Piper, looking insufferably pleased with himself. He came into the carriage. 'Isn't this just the strangest coincidence? I saw your names on the trunks in the van. I'm going across to New York too. I'll be sailing on the *Olympic* with you.' He smiled widely at them. 'I guess we'll have a lot to talk about.'

―――――

'Why Greece?' said Angela, as the train sped across the French countryside towards Switzerland.

'Why not?' replied Edgar. 'It's beautiful, sunny, reasonably civilized, and allows us to put several thousand miles between ourselves and that pestiferous press-man.'

'I wonder if we'll ever see our luggage again. I was rather looking forward to wearing that frock I bought at Madame Cousineau's,' she said regretfully. 'Now I expect it will spend the next month at Cherbourg and get crushed beyond repair.'

'You can always get a new one.'

'You know, if you'd only given me a *little* more warning of what you intended to do…'

'There wasn't time. The Athens train was about to depart, and if we hadn't made a bolt for it as soon as his back was turned we'd never have shaken him off. I don't know about you, but I didn't exactly relish the thought of having him lurking around corners and listening at our cabin door all the way across the Atlantic.'

'I suppose not. What do you think he said when he realized we'd given him the slip?'

'Something furious and unrepeatable, I imagine— which thought gives me great comfort.'

They laughed and he said, 'I'm sorry, darling. Not exactly how I intended things to happen. It seems fate meant us to have a honeymoon after all.'

'Well, we'll just have to do our best to enjoy it,' said Angela.

Chapter Two

PHILIP HALLIDAY SAT at a table on the terrace of the Hotel Acropolis, gazing idly out at the view, which was a fine one. To the right of him was a quaint little rocky harbour in which two or three fishing-boats bobbed merrily, their paint glinting brightly in the late afternoon sun, while to the left was the hotel swimming-pool, three sides of which were carved out of rock, with one side half-open to the sea. Beyond the pool a narrow stretch of golden sand could just be glimpsed, hemmed in by high cliffs that ended in a headland. Rising grandly on the hill behind him were the ruins of the acropolis which had given the hotel its name. The sky behind its shattered columns was the deepest of blues. It was a view to gladden the heart of any artist, but Philip Halliday was not an artist: he was an author—the notebook on the table in front of him declared it to be so. Never mind that he had bought it three weeks ago in Athens and its pages were still pristine, unblemished by so much as a drop of ink on the first page. It was a talisman; as long as he carried it he could remind himself of his true purpose in life. Here in

Rhodes was inspiration, he was sure of it—how could such sights and sounds and scents fail to move his imagination? The island held so many stories that had yet to be told. The story of the Knights Hospitaller, for example, who had made their home on Rhodes for two hundred years, from the fourteenth to the sixteenth centuries. Or, more recently, that peasant and his wife he had seen at the market today engaged in a noisy dispute. They had stood, blocking the street, for a good five minutes, he bellowing and gesticulating, she pointing a sharp finger at him and giving as good as she received. Another woman had eventually stepped in to intercede on behalf of the wife, which ended the argument—although not in the way the would-be mediator had presumably hoped, for they had both immediately turned upon her and berated her loudly. She retired, abashed, upon which the peasant and his wife had continued on their way. There was the beginning of something, the hint of a deeper truth. An idea sparked faintly within Philip and he picked up his pen.

'Isn't this weather delightful, Mr. Halliday!' came a loud female voice.

A feeling of cold dread stole over him, followed by a flash of annoyance, then resignation. There was no escape. He put down his pen again. The voice was attached to a hearty woman with a pink face and damp, wispy fair hair who was wheeling an elderly invalid in a chair.

'Lady Trenoweth, Miss Brinkhurst,' said Philip, in unenthusiastic greeting.

'You won't mind if we join you, will you?' said the woman with the carrying voice. 'No, no, there's no need to get up, I can manage quite well. There, now. Oh dear, you've dropped your rug, Lady Trenoweth. Let me put it back for you.'

'I don't need it,' snapped the invalid. 'It's quite hot enough.'

The other ignored her, tucking the blanket ruthlessly around her knees, then sat down at the table and beamed at Philip.

'Do go back to your writing. Don't mind us. It's just that this table is Lady Trenoweth's favourite spot on the terrace, and she mustn't be denied. Doctor's orders.'

'It's not my favourite spot at all,' said Lady Trenoweth. 'I'd rather be indoors. The sea air disagrees with me. I don't know why we came here in the first place. This hotel looks half-finished.'

'It's just the local style—without clutter, you know, to let the air pass through and keep the place cool.'

'I want to go back to the Grand Hotel in Rhodes. At least they have some idea of comfort, even if they are Italians.'

'Now, you know there were no suitable rooms available. This place is much quieter, and better for your health. I'll order you some tea.'

'I hate tea,' said the invalid.

Tea was eventually procured, and despite Lady Trenoweth's assertions, accepted grudgingly. Miss Brinkhurst leaned over, trying to get a glimpse of Philip's notebook.

'A beautiful spot for writing, isn't it? How is the novel going?'

'Very well, thank you,' lied Philip, putting away the notebook smoothly.

'So exciting, meeting a famous author! I must look up your books. I often read to Lady Trenoweth, and we have a fine time, don't we, Lady Trenoweth?'

'Your voice is too loud and flat. You have no idea of expression,' said Lady Trenoweth.

Miss Brinkhurst gave a wide smile.

'Naturally I don't speak as softly as you do.' Whether the remark were from obliviousness or malice could not be said, but it must have been one or the other, for her charge's voice was harsh and querulous from years of ill-health and ill-temper. 'We've just finished *The Good Companions* and enjoyed it thoroughly, didn't we, Lady Trenoweth?'

'I thought it amateurish,' replied that redoubtable invalid.

The two women appeared distinctly unsuited as companions. Philip wondered, not for the first time, why Miss Brinkhurst stayed in the employ of a woman who was so determined to be disagreeable—and indeed, why Lady Trenoweth had employed the nurse in the first place, since she evidently found her irritating.

Miss Brinkhurst, however, seemed unaffected by her charge's resolute peevishness. She was gazing across the terrace, where two men of middle age were sitting in close conversation over some notes. They were both very dusty. One of them, who was short with iron-grey hair, and by his tendency to gesticulate, unmistakably Italian, was holding forth with authority, while the other, a thin, nervous-looking man wearing round spectacles, nodded occasionally.

'I wonder whether they have found anything more at the dig today,' said Miss Brinkhurst. 'Professor Delisi told me they found a very fine amphora on Monday, virtually undamaged. He says the governor wants it to put on display at his residence. So fascinating to be here while history is practically being made! Only think how long all these objects have been buried! For centuries they have been hidden out of sight, but now we can see them again thanks to the efforts of the professor and Dr. Schulz.'

'Hmph. Foreigners!' was Lady Trenoweth's only contribution.

Miss Brinkhurst prattled on, ignoring Lady Trenoweth's irascible rejoinders. As she talked, a young woman came out onto the terrace. She was dark-haired, with warm, golden skin, deep-set, flashing eyes, and a sulky mouth, and had the sort of beauty that was capable of causing a lull in conversation whenever she arrived. Philip Halliday drew in his breath involuntarily, then frowned at himself. Even Miss Brinkhurst was spurred into momentary silence. Professor Delisi greeted the woman with an affectionate and proprietary air, and she sat down with him and his companion at their table. Miss Brinkhurst resumed her stream of conversation.

'Mrs. Delisi doesn't care to join her husband on the dig, I notice. I wonder whether she isn't a little bored. He must be twenty or thirty years older than she is. What does she do all day while he is away?'

'The same as the rest of us, I imagine,' said Philip. 'Sits half-dozing in the sun.'

'Young Mr. Cavell seems very *solicitous* towards her,' observed Miss Brinkhurst slyly. 'They spend a lot of time in company together. I expect the professor has asked him to take care of her when he's not there.'

She looked at Philip for encouragement, but he was not inclined to be drawn into any ill-natured speculation, and she went on:

'I suppose Miss Grayson doesn't mind Mr. Cavell's friendship with Mrs. Delisi, even though they *are* engaged. I did think I'd noticed a slight coolness between them yesterday, although I expect I was mistaken.'

'Spiteful old cat,' thought Philip, although he had noticed the same thing.

A waiter had approached the Delisis' table, and the

professor could be heard commanding a drink for his wife. Mrs. Delisi smiled at the waiter—such a smile as must have captivated the heart of any young man.

'She's bad luck,' said Philip to himself, although he was not usually a superstitious man.

He kept watching and caught sight of the waiter making a spitting motion with his mouth and crossing himself after Mrs. Delisi had turned away from him. It appeared the waiter agreed with Philip's assessment.

'Curious,' thought Philip.

Meanwhile, Lady Trenoweth and Miss Brinkhurst had launched into a dispute about their continued presence on the terrace and had not observed the little scene. At length Lady Trenoweth emerged victorious, so Miss Brinkhurst rose and began to fuss and bustle.

'We shall no doubt see you at dinner,' she said to Philip.

Then the two ladies departed and Philip watched as Miss Brinkhurst deliberately and viciously banged Lady Trenoweth's wheelchair against the door-frame as they went inside.

———

'I THOUGHT you said you were going to be civilized about this,' said Roy Cavell.

'How can I be civilized about it?' demanded Esther Grayson desperately, as she hurried after him up the road, shielding her eyes against the sun. 'I feel just the same about you as I always did—I can't help it. If it was just that you were tired of me, maybe I could bear it better. But to see you with her, following her around like a dog, tears my heart to pieces. Sometimes I feel I'd rather be dead than have to watch it day after day!'

'Don't talk like that! You know you don't mean it.'

'Yes I do. It's almost as if she's put some kind of spell on you. You can't keep your eyes off her.'

'You're being ridiculous.'

She ignored him and went on:

'It's easy to see why, but I didn't think you were the type to fall for it.'

'Fall for what? I haven't fallen for anything. Sophia's a nice kid, but there's nothing between us. Besides, in case you hadn't noticed, she's married.'

'Do you think she cares about that? Why, the professor's thirty years older than she is. I don't know why she married him, but she can't possibly be in love with him. She's the sort who drives men mad, Roy. She'll drive you mad. She's got you twisted around her finger. You don't think she really wants you, do you?'

'For the last time—'

'She's bad luck. There's an evil hanging about her, I can feel it!'

'Stop it, Esther! You're crazy.'

'Am I? Yes, I feel I must be sometimes, but then once in a while I start to think I'm the only sane one in this place. There's something wrong here, I can feel it. The professor suspects what's going on, anyway. That's why he's sending you to Athens. He wants you away from his wife.'

'That's not true.'

'Then why couldn't he have gone himself?'

'He's needed here at the dig.'

'Dr. Schulz can manage perfectly well without him. You ought to be careful, Roy. You don't get to the professor's position in life without having a ruthless streak, and he won't like you taking Sophia away from him. I've heard rumours about things that happened to other men who got too close to her. Ask her what happened in Salonika—go on, I dare you.'

Roy turned to her suddenly.

'Will you please stop talking about Sophia? I told you there's nothing going on and I meant it. Look, I'm sorry things ended between us, I truly am. But we couldn't go ahead with it, don't you see? What kind of a marriage would it be without love?'

'I have love enough for both of us,' said Esther in a small voice.

He shook his head.

'It would never have worked.' He sighed. 'Listen, Esther, why don't you go home? There's nothing for you here. Go back to the States, find someone else, forget about me.'

'You can't wait to get rid of me, is that it?'

'Of course not, but I hate to see you miserable. Do you think I'm happy about all this?'

For a moment they stared at one another, then she gestured wildly and burst out:

'I wish she hadn't come here. I wish we'd never set eyes on her. Then we would have finished our work here at the dig, gone back to the States and got married just like we always planned to. We would have been happy, I know it. But now it's all ruined, all because of Sophia Delisi.'

'I told you, it has nothing to do with Sophia,' he replied impatiently. He glanced at his watch. 'I'd better go and get my things. The taxi will be coming soon.'

He turned and set off up the path to the hotel.

'You'll regret it!' she called after him desperately.

———

Sophia Delisi was sitting alone on a sofa in a private corner of the hotel lounge when Roy Cavell came and planted himself in front of her.

16

'Have you thought about what I said?' he demanded abruptly.

'I've already told you, I cannot,' she replied. 'Why do you keep asking?'

'Because I won't believe it. I can't let you go, Sophia.'

'But you must.'

He pulled up a chair to face her and sat in it.

'I guess you're used to this—this dangling men on a string, but I won't stand for being dangled. You're coming with me to Athens, d'you hear? After that we'll go anywhere you like, but I won't go without you.'

She regarded him pityingly.

'Why must you make trouble?'

'I can't help it. You're all I think about. I don't know what you've done to me and I hate it, but I do know that I can't live without you.'

'Please leave me alone.'

'Is it the money? Is that it? You don't want to leave the comfort of life with the professor. I can make money. I have a rich pal from college who'll give me a job any time I ask for it, and it'll pay well too. He sent me a letter from London a couple of weeks ago, as a matter of fact. He wants me to come and work for him.' He spoke eagerly. 'This archaeology business was only ever a hobby, but I'm ready to settle down to a real job now and look after you properly. Come and see what life's like in America. You'll love it, and they'll love you there.' She was shaking her head, and he went on, 'Why do you stay here with him? He's old and ugly. You could snap your fingers and have any man, but you chose him. Why?'

'Perhaps I love him.'

'I don't believe that for a second. You don't mean that. I thought you loved me.'

'Then you were mistaken. I am sorry.'

He moved to take her hands in his but she slapped him away, glancing around.

'You're afraid somebody will see, is that it? Well I don't care who sees how I feel for you.'

'Not even Esther?'

'She'll come round,' he said unconvincingly.

'You think so? I think she will kill you rather than lose you.'

'Don't be ridiculous. Listen, Sophia—'

She put up a hand.

'I cannot listen to you,' she said. 'Please leave me alone. I have a headache. Go away.'

'But—'

'I cannot give you what you want. I don't know what you thought I would do, but there was never any question of my leaving Aldo.'

'Then there was never anything in it? You were leading me on all along?'

'I have never led you on. I never said anything I did not mean. I cannot help it if you chose to believe more than there was.'

She spoke with finality.

'You really mean it, don't you?' he said.

'Yes.'

He seemed bewildered, and for a moment looked rather like a small child who has broken his favourite toy.

'But what am I to do?'

'Go to Athens,' she replied. 'Aldo wants you to speak to the people at the Archaeological School, yes? Go there and talk about broken pots and statues and dead people, and forget about all this for a few days. You will wake up and realize you have been caught up in a kind of madness, and then you will come back here and everything will be nice again. We will call each other Mr. Cavell and Mrs. Delisi, as we did before, and we will forget this conversation.'

'You don't believe that any more than I do.' But he saw that she had made up her mind. 'Then you really won't come with me?'

She shook her head. He was about to argue but a clock chimed somewhere just then and he came to himself.

'I have to go, but if you think I'm going to get over all this in a few days you're very much mistaken, Sophia. I'm going to talk to Bill this evening about giving me that job, then I'll be back next week and we'll speak about this again. I won't be put off. You're the only woman I want, and I can't stand the thought of living without you.'

'You will be much better off without me. I will only bring you bad luck,' she said sadly. 'I bring nothing but bad luck.'

———

PROFESSOR DELISI GREETED his wife when she came down to breakfast the next morning.

'You are late to the dig today,' she said, as she joined him at the table.

'Yes, Schulz went into Rhodes to get some supplies and has not returned yet. No matter, you and I will have breakfast together. How is your head?'

'Better.'

'You must take care of yourself, my dear. Kostis!' He gestured to the waiter. Their order taken, he said:

'And so Cavell has gone off to Athens. Did he leave without a fuss?'

'How should I know?'

'I thought you sent him away.'

'Perhaps, but I did not pack his things myself or watch him go.'

'Did you not want to go with him?'

'Of course not. My place is here with you.'

'I thought the force of his arguments might change your mind.'

'He was very persistent,' she conceded.

'It is understandable. You draw them in like flies to honey, and sometimes they stick a little, eh? But don't worry. If he bothers you then I will see to him for you.'

'There will be no need for that.'

The professor caressed his wife's cheek approvingly.

'You are a good girl. He will be no trouble,' he said.

———

Miss Brinkhurst and Lady Trenoweth were just setting out to take a turn in the morning air before the sun rose too high, when a battered-looking motor-car came up the road and stopped at the Hotel Acropolis. Dr. Schulz alighted, together with two people Miss Brinkhurst did not recognize, a man and a woman.

'No, no, not at all!' the German archaeologist was saying earnestly. 'The taxis here are shocking, and I was coming this way anyway. You will like the Hotel Acropolis, I think. St. Michael is quieter than Rhodes, but you see the road is new and the hotel has all the modern conveniences for tourists. You must try the swimming-pool. It is quite sheltered and the water is a very pleasant temperature. Now, you must excuse me, as I am late, and Professor Delisi is waiting for me.'

'New guests,' said Miss Brinkhurst pleasurably, as a porter came out to take care of the luggage and the newcomers stood, looking about them. 'I wonder who they are. They look very smart.'

'*Too* smart if you ask me. Flashy. Clothes too sharply pressed—and look at those new suitcases. No better than they ought to be, I expect,' replied Lady Trenoweth as the little party went indoors.

'Oh, but they must be quite forty.'

'Once a sinner always a sinner.'

'I dare say you would know,' said Miss Brinkhurst vaguely. 'They sounded English. That will make a nice change from all the Americans and foreigners. Sometimes I feel as though we're quite in the minority. The woman looked familiar. I have the feeling I've seen her somewhere before. He called her Angela. Well, I shall find out all about them as soon as I can.'

'Heaven help them,' muttered Lady Trenoweth.

Chapter Three

THEIR ROOM WOULD NOT BE ready for an hour or so, they were told, but Mr. Florakis, the manager of the Hotel Acropolis, suggested that in the meantime Mr. and Mrs. Merivale might like to take coffee on the terrace—or, if they preferred, there was a path a little way up the road which, after a short and not too taxing walk, led to a very fine view of the bay. Angela and Edgar decided upon the latter.

'It will do us good to stretch our legs,' said Edgar as they walked. 'Besides, there was a hefty female loitering about with a gleam in her eye. I know the type. She'd have followed us onto the terrace and pumped us dry of information in ten minutes flat if we'd stayed.'

'The nurse pushing the woman in the wheelchair, you mean? Yes, I saw her too. We'll have to face her at some point, I expect.'

The road was steeper than Mr. Florakis had given them to believe, and Angela stopped for a moment to fetch her breath and look out through a gap between two houses which gave a tantalizing glimpse of the sea beyond.

'It really is beautiful,' she said. 'I'm glad you suggested we come here. Athens was a fine city, but too noisy and smelly. The air here has a heavenly scent to it. What is it?'

'Rosemary, I should say,' he replied, indicating a nearby bush. He pulled off a handful of spiky leaves and held them under her nose. 'Here.'

She breathed them in.

'Yes that's it. Lovely.'

The road climbed ever upward, passing a small patch of trees through which more glimpses of the sea could be seen. Then at last it emerged onto a sort of rocky plateau, giving a fine vista of the Aegean and the outline of the Anatolian coast beyond it. Below them was the harbour with its brightly coloured boats, and the hotel with its swimming-pool carved out of the rock, while if they turned their heads they could see the acropolis looming behind them, with three or four mountain-goats grazing in the ruins. A bench was on the plateau, put there quite recently by the looks of it, and they sat to take in the sun and absorb the scenery. It was almost the first moment they had had to themselves since Paris, and a short silence fell. At last Angela turned her eyes away from the view to find Edgar looking at her quizzically.

'Well, here we are,' she said, for it seemed as though some remark were needed.

'Here we are indeed. I've done my time and you're mine at last. What shall I do with you now I've got you?'

'Treat me nicely and don't lie to me more than you can help. And in return I promise to plague you as little as possible.'

He looked amused.

'Very well.'

They shook hands on it, and Angela laughed.

'A gentleman's agreement. Not exactly romantic, is it? I

imagine other people swear undying love and devotion to one another, or something of the sort.'

'We can do that too, if you like.'

'Is that necessary? A little vulgar, perhaps, like a scene from a sixpenny novel. Let's take it as read.'

'Not regretting it, I hope?'

'Of course not. Why should I regret it?'

'What if someone finds out who you're married to, or another news-hound turns up?'

'Oh, they won't here, surely?'

'Perhaps not, but it won't be so easy to hide when we go back. As you know only too well, one's past has the nasty habit of catching up with one.'

'I don't want to hide,' said Angela. 'I promised I wouldn't deny you, don't you remember? That was part of the bargain.'

'Yes, it was.'

'And I shall keep my promise.'

'I'm glad to hear it.' He eyed her speculatively. 'So then, now that we've concluded our gentleman's agreement I suppose I'm allowed to kiss you? Is that included in the terms?'

Angela glanced around.

'Well, gentlemen don't generally kiss one another, but since there's nobody about I'm prepared to make an exception in this case.'

'Thank you,' said Edgar gravely.

A few minutes later a peasant leading a donkey approached up the path to find a foreign lady and gentleman sitting slightly apart on the bench, not looking at one another, the lady in the act of straightening her frock. He stared at them curiously and passed on.

'It appears to be impossible to escape an audience,' remarked Edgar.

Angela gazed up at the acropolis behind them.

'I wonder how one gets up there. It's not as grand as the one in Athens, of course, but I'd like to go and see it. We might visit Lindos too and see the fortress. What Dr. Schulz was telling us about the Knights of St. John was fascinating.'

'You prefer that period to antiquity?'

'One feels more connected with more recent times, I suppose. The ancient Greeks were so long ago that they seem almost like a different species, but the Christian era is something that's more familiar.'

'Very well,' he said. 'We'll go to Lindos and wander around the ruins and find a guide to explain it all to us.'

The sun was higher in the sky now, and they had drunk their fill of the view.

'It's getting rather hot up here,' said Angela. 'Do you think our room is ready yet?'

Edgar glanced at his watch.

'If it isn't we'll go and make a nuisance of ourselves until it is,' he replied.

He stood up and held out a hand. She took it, and they walked back down the hill together.

———

As PREDICTED, Miss Brinkhurst waylaid them later when they entered the dining-room where afternoon tea was being served.

'Mr. and Mrs. Merivale, isn't it?' she hallooed. 'I am Amy Brinkhurst. You will join me, won't you?'

They would much rather not have, but Miss Brinkhurst had called out so loudly that it was difficult to escape without looking rude.

'How does she know our name?' whispered Angela as

they walked towards Miss Brinkhurst's table, where she was sitting alone. 'Do you think she stole the hotel register?'

'I expect she got Mr. Florakis in a half nelson and refused to let him go until he told her,' replied Edgar.

They sat down and formal introductions were made. Miss Brinkhurst said:

'So nice to meet new people. We saw you arrive this morning, but missed you at luncheon. Rhodes is a beautiful place, isn't it? There is so much to see, and so many places to visit! What have you been doing today?'

'Making up for lost time, mostly,' murmured Edgar.

Angela tapped his ankle sharply with her foot under the table.

'It's been a long journey and we were hot and tired, so we haven't been out yet,' she said. 'But we thought we might go for a dip in the pool before dinner.'

'Well, I'm glad you have chosen to brighten up our little company. But why St. Michael in particular? Most people prefer to stay in the old town.'

'As a matter of fact, we were planning to stay in Rhodes, but the Grand Hotel was full so they recommended this place to us.'

'That was quite right of them. This is the next best hotel on the island, and St. Michael is a very pretty little village and handy for Rhodes itself—only a short drive away on the new road. The Italians have made many improvements since they occupied the island. I gather they are developing Rhodes with the intention of attracting tourists, and one can certainly understand why. The climate in particular is very beneficial.'

She then proceeded to examine them thoroughly in the matter of their place of origin, their respective families, Edgar's profession, their journey, their intended length of stay (with sundry hinted queries about whether they could afford it), Angela's clothes (ditto), their opinion of foreigners, particularly Greeks and Italians, and—somewhat oddly—whether they had ever visited Baden-Baden. They politely withstood the grilling without giving anything away except to say that they lived near New York and travelled frequently. Miss Brinkhurst saw that a direct approach had been the wrong one, and, disappointed in her attempts to tear the meat from the bone, changed tack and began picking at the scraps around the edge.

'And so Dr. Schulz brought you here?' she said.

'Yes,' replied Angela. 'We met him in Rhodes this morning and happened to mention we were coming here, and he very kindly offered to bring us in his car, as the taxis at the Grand Hotel were all busy.'

'Such a clever man, and most polite. Has he been telling you about the dig? It's not far from here, and the Hotel Acropolis is a sort of base for all the archaeologists.'

'Yes, he did mention it. It sounded very interesting.'

'Well, then, you must get Professor Delisi to invite you to visit it one day.'

'Who is Professor Delisi? I believe I've heard the name.'

'He is head of the Archaeological School in Athens, and has been sent by the Italian government to take charge of all the excavations on the island. He's very well respected in his field. Do you remember the discovery of the Peraia Bronzes a few years ago? He was the one who found them.'

'Oh, that was Professor Delisi, was it? Yes, I remember reading about it at the time.'

'Dr. Schulz is his assistant. He is from a German university—I forget which. Then we have the two young Americans, Mr. Cavell and Miss Grayson, who are also working at the dig, although Mr. Cavell has gone off to

Athens for a week, so I don't suppose you'll get to meet him, which is a pity.'

'Where exactly is the dig?' Angela wanted to know. 'Can we walk there?'

'It's not more than two or three miles from here, up in the hills, but a little too far to walk in this hot weather. It is a mediaeval fortress with some Hellenistic remains nearby. I don't pretend to understand it all myself but the professor explained it very nicely.'

'Is everyone here an archaeologist?'

'Oh, not at all. No, Lady Trenoweth and I are merely tourists. We originally intended to go to Baden-Baden— that's why I wondered if you knew anything of it—but somebody told us the climate in Rhodes would be very beneficial to Lady Trenoweth's health, so we came here instead.'

A man with dark, deep-set eyes and an air of suppressed nervous energy entered the dining-room. He nodded at them but passed on and went out onto the terrace before Miss Brinkhurst could waylay him and insist he join their party.

'That's Philip Halliday, the author,' she confided. 'He is here writing a book. He's very polite. I told him I should have to be careful, in case I end up a character in his story! He insisted I needn't worry, but one never knows, does one?' She let out a laugh that was a sort of braying hoot.

They watched as Halliday spoke pleasantly to a forlorn-looking young woman who was sitting at a table outside, and joined her at her invitation.

'And *that* is Esther Grayson, whom I just mentioned,' said Miss Brinkhurst. 'She went to one of these modern American women's colleges, where they study night and day until they ruin their eyesight. In my day we used to call them blue-stockings. She and young Mr. Cavell are supposed to have an understanding, although I suspect it has come to an end in recent days.' Upon Angela's inquiring look she dropped her voice and said, 'One doesn't like to gossip, but it's become rather obvious that Mr. Cavell has developed an unfortunate infatuation for his employer's wife.'

'Goodness!' said Angela, since an answer was evidently expected of her.

Miss Brinkhurst affected an air of delicacy.

'Mrs. Delisi is a *certain kind* of woman, and not the sort to refuse the attentions of a young man—although to be perfectly frank, one can't wonder that Mr. Cavell might have fallen into temptation, since Miss Grayson won't tear herself away from her books. Gentlemen don't like ladies who are too intellectual, do they, Mr. Merivale?'

'Oh, I can't bear clever women. Luckily Angela's practically a half-wit, aren't you, darling?' replied Edgar.

'Dear me!' exclaimed Miss Brinkhurst, regarding him uncertainly.

Fortunately, the waiter just then arrived with tea.

'Stop it!' hissed Angela while Miss Brinkhurst's attention was distracted. Edgar assumed a look of innocence, but decided it was wiser to behave himself. He helped Miss Brinkhurst to sugar and proceeded to be charming for the next five minutes.

'Such a pity Lady Trenoweth isn't here to meet you,' said Miss Brinkhurst. 'But she is at present having her afternoon nap. She needs her rest, for she is quite an invalid.'

'Was Lady Trenoweth the lady in the wheelchair we saw earlier?'

'Yes. I'm by way of being a sort of nurse-companion. It's not what I was brought up to, but my family came down in the world some years ago and now I must earn my living. However, I'm pleased to say I'm not at all a snob, and I like to be busy, so I don't bemoan my lot. Lady Trenoweth and I are from the same part of the world, and I knew her slightly as a child, although she's a good deal older than I. She was Adela Ford, you know—the famous society beauty. She was very much the thing at the turn of the century. I expect you've seen the portrait of her by Sargent. Sadly invalided now, of course, and the sickness has taken away all her looks. Such a tragedy.'

She paused to sip her tea complacently, looking wholly unmoved by her employer's travails despite her words.

A man with thinning hair and clothes that did not quite fit him entered the dining-room and was shown to a table. He fussed and fidgeted with his chair and his napkin, then ordered tea, accompanied by a long list of instructions as to exactly how it should be served.

'Another new guest,' said Miss Brinkhurst. 'American, I should say.'

'They're certainly doing a good job of attracting the tourists,' said Angela.

Miss Brinkhurst soon afterwards had to go and see to Lady Trenoweth, so took her leave with many salutations and much insistence that they should all sit together at dinner.

'Remind me to go mysteriously deaf and blind next time she invites us to join her at her table,' said Edgar, once she had gone. 'I feel as though I'd been given the third degree. Why do women of that sort always have a laugh like a braying donkey?'

'It was very *carrying*, shall we say,' agreed Angela. A thought struck her. 'I don't laugh like a donkey, do I?'

'Your laugh is as delightful as the rest of you,' he assured her.

'How very kind of you to say so. You know, you're

wasted on horses. You ought to go into the diplomatic corps.'

'What, and have to be polite to people like the Brinkhurst all day long? What a horrible thought! Horses are much easier—my word, who's that?' he said suddenly.

He was looking through the open glass doors to the terrace as he spoke. Angela turned to follow his gaze, and saw what they had not noticed before—a young woman who had been sitting alone with her back to them in a quiet corner of the terrace, and who had now stood up. She entered the dining-room and swayed through quite unselfconsciously, as several people glanced up. Angela watched her retreat, startled.

'Goodness, she's a beauty, isn't she? Who is that lady?' she asked, as the waiter came to clear away their things.

'It is Mrs. Delisi,' replied the young man.

'The famous destroyer of engagements, I presume,' said Angela, once the waiter had gone.

'I can see why,' replied Edgar, watching Mrs. Delisi go likewise.

'Well, tear your eyes away if you can and let's go and bathe.'

———

ON INQUIRING of the hotel manager, they were informed that the pool was perfectly safe, although on windy days they were to be careful on approaching the side close to the entrance to the sea, for the waves had been known to carry people over the rocks and out into open water. In this event there was little danger for a strong swimmer, Mr. Florakis hastened to add, for the currents hereabouts were not so powerful as to be hazardous; it was just that the water in the sea was colder and not so pleasant.

They were the only people at the pool, which sloped naturally upwards at the shore end, with a floor that was part sand, part flat rocks perfect for sitting on in the shallows. The sun had been hot all day, but a breeze had got up in the afternoon and the temperature was pleasantly comfortable.

'That's a very fetching bathing-suit,' said Edgar. 'Where did you get it? Athens?'

'No, Rhodes, this morning, while you were arguing with the customs people about the luggage.'

'So that's where you disappeared to. Never miss an opportunity, do you?'

'Oh, but it was in the window and I couldn't possibly resist it. Besides, I left all my things on the train, you may remember, and they had to be replaced.'

'Don't tell me you brought a bathing-suit to meet me at Clairvaux.'

'No, perhaps not. I will concede that this particular garment is not a replacement as such. Still, I'm glad you like it.' Angela introduced a foot gingerly into the water. 'It's not cold at all!' she said in surprise. 'Beautifully warm, in fact.'

She sat lazily in the shallows, watching as Edgar swam widths with a notable display of energy. The left and right sides of the pool were man-made, with smooth, flat paths around them and a ladder set into the wall to the left, while the fourth side was formed from a natural outcrop that partly closed off the pool from the sea. The outcrop dipped steeply in the middle, so that one section of it was under the water. As Mr. Florakis had said, it would be easy to swim or float across it and out into the open sea. Angela closed her eyes, enjoying the heat of the sun, then opened them again suddenly as several drops of water flicked across her face. It was Edgar.

'Must you?' she said.

'You were falling asleep.'

'No I wasn't. I was just thinking.'

'About what?'

As a matter of fact, she had been thinking about another bathing-suit she had seen in the same shop in Rhodes, and wondering whether it was worth the trip back to buy it.

'Never mind,' she replied, and struck out of the shallows to get away from him, since he was demonstrating a troublesome inclination to continue splashing her.

Further out, the water became deeper and the bottom less sandy. The waves in the pool were gentle ones, in contrast to the choppiness she could see through the gap in the rocks. A large boat was passing close to the shore—perhaps a pleasure cruiser. She turned and waved to Edgar, who had taken her place on the rock in the shallows, then rolled onto her back and began swimming slowly up and down the pool, thinking of nothing much, but merely enjoying the feeling of the water on her skin. An unwelcome wave broke nearby and slopped across her face, and she stopped to shake her head, grimacing. The boat's passage had begun to cause peaks and troughs in the water, carrying Angela up and down with them, so she swam towards the outcrop, where there was a useful hand-hold, to wait for the disturbance to pass. Here at the far end of the pool the sea was not so pleasant: it was colder and darker, with a stronger current. The water sloshed and swirled and sucked against the rocks as the cruiser chugged onwards. As she trod water, waiting for the waves to calm before striking out again, Angela felt a patch of seaweed brush unpleasantly against her foot. She moved away, peering into the water, and saw that the seaweed was drifting up towards the surface, presumably dislodged by the passing boat. This part of the pool was certainly to be avoided. She would return to the shallows.

A strange looking kind of seaweed, however, and not one she had seen before. It was solid and bulky, and had felt odd against her foot. *Was* it seaweed?

Angela looked again, and what she saw made her turn cold. Jerking sharply away from the rocks she let out a little shriek, and in doing so took in a mouthful of salt water. She coughed and spluttered, but her only thought was to get away from the thing she had seen. She ploughed desperately towards the side of the pool, ignoring the stinging of the salt water in her eyes, grabbed at the ladder thankfully and shot up it onto the flat carved rock, where she stood, white in the face and gasping for air.

Edgar had seen something was wrong. He ran along the side of the pool towards her and thumped her on the back until she got over the coughing fit.

'What is it?' he demanded, once she had got her breath back. 'Are you all right? I've never seen you move so fast.'

She raised her eyes to him in horror.

'There's something in the sea!' she exclaimed. 'Oh Edgar, I think it's a man!'

Chapter Four

THEY LOOKED for as long as they could, until the sun was low on the horizon and Angela's teeth were chattering, but whatever it was she had seen had either subsided out of sight or washed over the rocks into the sea, for they found nothing.

'Are you quite sure?' said Edgar, for perhaps the twentieth time. 'You don't think you might have been imagining it?'

'I'm not in the habit of imagining things,' replied Angela crossly. 'But no, I can't be completely sure it was a man. I suppose it might have been some dead sea creature. It's just it did look awfully human.'

'Well, there's no use in our staying here now—it's starting to get dark and we'll only just be in time for dinner as it is. We'd better speak to Mr. Florakis about it.'

There was no question of their making a big fuss, for it would not do to frighten all the guests, but even so Mr. Florakis paled when they mentioned it to him, and they were forced to promise repeatedly that they would say nothing for the present.

'You understand, this is a new hotel and we do not want any unpleasantness,' he said. 'If the news gets out then we will have the authorities here, and they will bother the guests with questions, when it may be that what you saw has nothing to do with us. Somebody who fell overboard from a boat, perhaps.'

'But we can't just do nothing,' Angela objected.

'Naturally we must do something. But now you see it is dark, and what use is it to bring the *carabinieri* here when they will not be able to see? None of the guests will go into the pool for the next few hours, so I say far better to wait until tomorrow. I will send some men out to look in the morning as soon as it is light, and if we find anything then of course we will report it. But until then you will say nothing, yes?'

It was hardly an unreasonable request, so they agreed and went into dinner.

'You're rather quiet,' observed Edgar after a while. 'You're not too upset, are you? We can leave this place if you like.'

'That won't be necessary,' replied Angela. 'I'm not as feeble as all that. I got a shock, that's all. As a matter of fact, I was just wondering whether Mr. Florakis mightn't have been right about somebody falling from a boat. There was one passing at the time.'

'It was too far out. A body couldn't have floated from there into the pool that quickly.'

'No, I suppose not.' She shook herself and smiled. 'What a gruesome subject for dinner! Let's not think about it any more. If there's anything to find, then Mr. Florakis's men will find it and take it away.'

'They certainly won't leave it there in the swimming-pool,' agreed Edgar.

———

AFTER BREAKFAST the next morning Edgar disappeared on some mysterious errand of his own, and Angela was wavering between writing a postcard or two or going for a walk when Mr. Florakis approached her and said quietly:

'I sent two men out very early this morning, and they looked for more than an hour but found nothing in the pool.'

'Oh!'

'They searched very thoroughly, and it is not possible that they would have missed anything of the sort you mentioned,' he went on. 'So if you were correct in what you saw, it is certain that the current carried it over the rocks and out into the sea. I dare say it was some unfortunate sailor or fisherman. A Turk, perhaps.'

'What are the tides like here? Will it wash up somewhere along the coast?' Angela wanted to know.

Mr. Florakis shrugged.

'It is possible. Or it may be that he will drift out to sea and disappear forever. But without a body there is no cause to call the police.'

He was looking at her appealingly. Evidently he did not wish for any trouble to befall his hotel.

'I expect you're right,' said Angela, who was beginning to wonder whether she had seen a body at all. Perhaps it had been nothing more than a large clump of seaweed, with some debris from the beach tangled in among it, and the rough sea had made it look like something it was not. After all, she had only glimpsed it for a second before retreating as fast as possible. The thought relieved her somewhat, since she had not exactly relished the prospect of becoming mixed up with the Italian police. Edgar had done his sentence and was a free man now, but she was not so naive as to believe there were no other misdeeds in his past about which he had not told her. He would not thank her for attracting the attention of the authorities—and besides, regardless of all other considerations, a dead body would make an unwelcome third on their honeymoon.

After some hesitation she decided to write her post-cards, and went into the lobby, where Mr. Florakis was now being accosted by the fussy American who had arrived the day before.

'I am afraid it is not possible to give you a West-facing room,' the hotel manager was saying. 'The rooms here all face North or South.'

Passing through into the dining-room, Angela put her head out onto the terrace and immediately saw the familiar figure of Miss Brinkhurst arranging a rug over the knees of her elderly charge. They had not spotted her, and she with-drew hurriedly, deciding that the reading-room would be nicely private. But when she entered she found someone else had got there before her, and was engaged in writing a letter at the only desk. It was Esther Grayson, the girl whom Miss Brinkhurst had suggested was such a fearsome intellectual that she had driven her fiancé into the arms of another woman.

'Excuse me,' said Angela, preparing to withdraw.

'Not at all, I'm nearly finished,' replied the girl. She scribbled a postscript and looked about for an envelope. Angela said pleasantly:

'You're Miss Grayson, aren't you? I understand you're one of the archaeological party.'

'That's right,' answered Esther Grayson. 'No secrets around here!'

The tone of the remark was bright and yet oddly bitter. Angela looked more closely and saw she had been crying.

'I do beg your pardon, I didn't mean to upset you.'

Two bright pink spots appeared on the girl's cheeks and tears began to form in the corners of her eyes. She swallowed.

'Don't be sorry. It's just that it's hard having everyone talking behind their hands about you wherever you go.' She saw Angela's uncertain look and went on, 'Oh, you needn't be coy about it. I saw you having tea with Miss Brinkhurst yesterday and knew what would follow. She takes great pleasure in making sure everybody knows everybody else's secrets.'

'Why, I...' began Angela, but Esther was collecting up her papers and preparing to leave.

'Don't listen to what that cat says,' she said savagely. 'She's the sort that's only happy when people are miserable. I'd watch out for her if I were you. She'll poke and pry until she worms every skeleton out of your closet, then she'll whisper them to everyone and gloat while she's doing it.'

On that note she left. Angela hesitated for a moment, then sat down.

'She is right,' came a voice.

Angela started, and looked up to see the beautiful young woman of the day before, who had been sitting unseen in a high-backed armchair facing the window. The woman threw a magazine aside and regarded Angela with interest.

'I saw you come yesterday,' she said. 'I am Sophia Delisi. And you are Mrs. Merivale.'

'That's right. You're with the dig too, aren't you?'

'No, I am not an archaeologist. I hate old things—they are so dull and dusty! But my husband likes them very much, so I come to be with him.'

'You stay here at the hotel while he sees to the excavations?'

'Mostly. Sometimes Aldo tells me he has found a beautiful statue or a pretty vase, or sometimes even a gold pendant, and I go along and see it to please him. But the thing is always cracked, or broken, or crushed, and the gold does not shine, and to me it is not beautiful. But I gasp and say, "How delightful, darling," and Aldo is very happy.'

'You are not Italian, I think?'

'No, I am Greek, from the North, near Salonika. That is where I met Aldo. He is very big and important and I was very poor, but he could not take his eyes off me.'

'That's quite understandable, if you don't mind my saying so.'

Sophia nodded.

'Yes, everyone likes to look at me, so it did not matter that I was poor. Money is not the only currency, you understand. I use what has been given to me.'

Her frankness was disarming.

'But don't you find it tiresome at times? Having people look at you, I mean.'

'Most of the time I do not notice it. But sometimes a man will bother me, and then Aldo takes care of it. He is a good husband,' she added, as though the question were in doubt. 'He protects me.'

'I'm pleased to hear it.'

'Your husband looks very nice. Does he protect you?'

Angela considered the question.

'We haven't been married long,' she replied at last, 'but I suppose he does. I doubt I need protecting in the same way as you, though.'

'No. You have been here only since yesterday, and the fat woman who pushes the ugly toad about in a chair has not found out anything about you yet to tell to all the other guests. But she will if she can, so keep your secrets to yourself.'

'I have every intention of it,' Angela assured her.

'Sooner or later she will tell you bad things about me, if she has not already, and perhaps you will believe them. I hope not.'

With that cryptic remark Mrs. Delisi smiled, rose, and left the room.

'Goodness me!' said Angela to herself.

She finished writing her postcards and went to buy stamps from the hotel reception desk. It was not yet ten o'clock, and Edgar had not returned, so she decided to take a walk after all. The small beach that was visible from the terrace looked particularly inviting, and she decided to go there. On coming out of the hotel she bumped into a handsome young Greek who was standing behind a large ornamental potted plant by the front entrance, furtively smoking a cigarette, and recognized him as one of the waiters. He threw the cigarette hurriedly into the pot and straightened up when he saw her.

'Kostis, isn't it?' said Angela.

He smiled widely.

'Yes, madam. How may I help you? You want to go to the market in St. Michael? It is not five minutes—straight ahead and turn right at the church. Or perhaps you want to go into Rhodes? My brother Yannis has a taxi and can take you.'

'I'd like to get down to that little beach I saw from the hotel. Is there a path?'

'Yes, madam. Just turn right here and walk for two minutes and you will see a sign in English pointing to Archangel Beach.'

'Archangel Beach? What an unusual name. Does it have to do with the name of the town?'

'Yes. There is a legend from a long time ago that says the Archangel Michael himself appeared before a fisherman on the beach. Or some stories say it was a child who saw him. But when the people here heard the story they built a church and then a village, and so this is called the beach of the Archangel. Whether the legend is true or not I cannot say, but the beach is pretty, and very sheltered for bathing. Here, I will show you the way.'

Ignoring her protests, he escorted her along a path that led down through a patch of scrubby bushes and out onto the beach in question, which was a strip of sand perhaps a quarter of a mile long that curved in a neat arc around towards a steep headland at one end, while at the other end was a small promontory on which the Hotel Acropolis was situated. The whole thing was surrounded by rocks that were just right for clambering about on or picnicking or sun-bathing, or all three. Kostis acknowledged her thanks with a brilliant smile then disappeared back up the path, and Angela went to stand by the water, looking out to sea. From here she could see people moving about on the hotel terrace, although it was too far away for her to recognize any of them. It was peaceful here, but she was not alone, for a little further along the shore was a man, pacing up and down a short stretch of beach by the water, staring at the sand as he walked, and muttering to himself. As he came towards her she saw it was the man who had been pointed out to her by Miss Brinkhurst as the author Philip Halliday. Deciding not to disturb him, she retreated further up the beach and began to walk in the direction away from the hotel.

It was perfectly natural for her to take a stroll here. If her route occasionally meandered into hollows and crevices among the rocks—why, that was only because she wanted to explore the rock-pools and look for stranded fish or the occasional crab. There was no reason at all to suppose she might find anything so horrid as a dead body. Of course, if someone *did* happen to have fallen overboard from a passing boat, and *did* happen to have floated into shore, this was exactly the sort of place they might wash up. Mr. Florakis had said the currents here were not especially powerful, so if a body *was* going to wash up anywhere it might easily be here, stranded in among the rocks. Here she caught herself.

'Angela, you ass, can't you even go on honeymoon without looking for trouble?' she said to herself.

She turned determinedly away from the rocks and headed back towards the sea. The sand was starting to collect uncomfortably in her shoes so she slipped them off and walked barefoot. There—now if she found herself drifting dangerously back towards the sharp rocks her feet would warn her off.

Philip Halliday was still pacing up and down a little way ahead, and as Angela watched she saw another man approach and walk alongside him. It was the American who had arrived the day before and had asked Mr. Florakis for a room with a West view. She seemed to remember his name was Peterson. She could not hear what they were saying, but the American was gesticulating animatedly, evidently determined to join Halliday on his walk. The two men set off together towards the headland and disappeared from view.

Wondering whether it were possible to skirt the headland and see what was beyond it, Angela decided to walk that way too. At a certain point the sand ended and she had no choice but to put her shoes back on in order to progress further. The rocks were low and flat and dry here, and it was easy to jump from one to another. Further along, however, towards the part of the headland that jutted out into the sea, they were damp and covered with large patches of seaweed. Angela proceeded across the rocks, looking for footholds and advancing gradually towards the headland. At length an obstacle arose in the shape of a particularly tall shelf of rock which was impossible to climb over. She would have to go around it. It was something of a struggle, and at one point she nearly slipped into a rock-pool, but at length she triumphed and found herself on the other side.

The first thing she saw was Philip Halliday, who was crouched down, peering at something which lay across a large patch of seaweed. At first glance it looked like a heap of abandoned clothes. Halliday's companion had turned away and was bending forward, his hand to his stomach.

'Oh dear, oh dear!' he was moaning.

Halliday turned and saw Angela. He stood up.

'Get back!' he commanded.

But it was too late, for she had already seen—had known full well what she would see, in fact.

Chapter Five

'Yes, I'm quite all right, thank you,' said Angela. 'But I'm not sure about your friend.'

The American was indeed looking very green, and kept his face turned determinedly away from the thing that had once been a man lying dead on the rocks.

'I'm sorry,' he said. 'It was just a shock to see it, that's all. Don't mind me.'

'It's not very pleasant, is it?' said Angela. After one glance she had not looked again.

'Drowned, by the looks of it. We'd better go and report it,' said Philip Halliday.

'Yes, the sooner we do that the sooner they can identify who it is,' she agreed.

Philip said grimly:

'Oh, I know who it is all right.'

'Really? Goodness me! Who?'

'His name's Roy Cavell. He is—or was—working with the archaeological fellows at the dig up in the hills.'

Angela glanced at him in surprise.

'Cavell? Yes, I've heard the name.' It was on the tip of

her tongue to say she had been introduced to Roy Cavell in the swimming-pool the day before, but on reflection she decided it was wiser to stay silent on the subject. 'How awful! What happened to him?'

'I'd very much like to know that myself. I saw him not two days ago and he was alive and kicking. As far as I knew he'd gone to Athens for a week. Clearly he never arrived.' As though drawn to it against his will, Halliday turned to look at the mortal remains of Roy Cavell. 'I knew she was bad luck,' he muttered.

'Who?' asked Angela.

He turned back to her and seemed to recollect himself.

'Never mind. I'm sorry, my name's Philip Halliday.'

'Angela Mar—Merivale,' said Angela.

'Not exactly the best start to the day, I'm afraid—I'm sorry you had to see it.'

'That's all right. You—you weren't out here looking for him, were you?' she asked hesitantly, for it had just occurred to her that given the ease with which Halliday had made his disturbing discovery, perhaps he had had good reason to think that Cavell might be here.

'Good Lord, no! Peterson here and I were just taking a turn on the rocks when we found him. I thought it was just a heap of seaweed at first, and got quite a shock once I realized what it really was. Poor devil.'

'Was Cavell a friend of yours?'

'Not particularly, but we'd had one or two drinks together.'

'I wonder how it happened,' said Angela.

'I expect he decided to have one last dip in the sea before he set off to Athens and got into difficulties.'

'But he's fully dressed,' Angela pointed out.

'Oh yes, he is, isn't he? Stupid of me. Well, then, I

don't know. I suppose the police will make inquiries about all that.'

Angela mused for a moment or two, frowning.

'When exactly did you last see him?' she asked.

'Monday afternoon, as I recall. He left for Rhodes on Monday evening—at least that's what he was meant to do. He was to catch the boat from there early on Tuesday.'

'And today is Wednesday,' said Angela. 'We arrived yesterday morning so must have just missed him. And some time between then and now he died.'

Mr. Peterson had pulled himself together now and was looking from Angela to Halliday.

'This poor man. What a terrible accident!' he said.

'I suppose it must have been,' replied Angela.

'Don't you agree?' Halliday asked in surprise.

'I have no idea. I'm just trying to think of a reason why he might have ended up in the sea rather than going to Rhodes. Did he change his mind at the last minute and decide to stay here? Why was he going to Athens, by the way?'

'Something to do with the dig, I think. Professor Delisi sent him.'

His tone was slightly too casual. Angela threw him a sharp glance but said nothing.

He went on:

'The whole thing's incomprehensible. Are you better now?' he demanded of the American.

'Yes, thank you. Just a little moment of weakness. So you knew this unfortunate man?'

'Yes—he was a guest at the hotel.'

'Good heavens!' said the other. 'This isn't the kind of thing I expected to happen on a quiet holiday,' he added, somewhat inadequately.

'No,' agreed Halliday. 'Well, no sense in waiting around here. There's nothing we can do for him now.'

They all turned and set off back towards the hotel. Angela and Philip soon outstripped Peterson, who was evidently not a hardy or athletic sort and was having trouble making his way over the rocks.

'Ought we to wait for him?' said Angela.

'He can find his own way back.' Philip glanced back at the other man, who had stopped to mop his brow and remove a stone from his shoe. 'As a matter of fact, he attached himself to me like a limpet this morning on the beach when I wanted to do some thinking on my own, and I couldn't shake him off because he was determined to tell me all about his trip to London and his visit to the Chelsea flower show. Well, much good it did him.'

'He did look rather ill,' agreed Angela.

'Serve him right,' said Philip callously.

Back at the hotel Angela left it to Halliday to report the bad news to Mr. Florakis, then went onto the terrace, which was quieter now, with no sign of Miss Brinkhurst or Lady Trenoweth—much to her relief, for she was sure the news would be all over the hotel soon, and she did not relish the thought of having to answer Miss Brinkhurst's ghoulish questions about the dead body on the beach.

She went to look out over the rail, towards the outcrop of rocks. The place where Roy Cavell's body lay could not be seen from here. Perhaps they ought to have left someone to wait with the body until help came—although there was little chance of its being washed away, for the sea was calm today. Looking at the view from where she stood, it was difficult to believe that such a disturbing thing could have happened in such beautiful surroundings. She sensed movement at her shoulder and turned to see that Mr.

Peterson had arrived back at last, and was bobbing about breathlessly next to her.

'I beg your pardon, I didn't introduce myself properly,' he said eagerly. 'John B. Peterson of the Peterson Oil Corporation—I guess you've heard of it. I'm not the original Peterson, of course—that was my grandfather. And you're Mrs. Merivale, isn't that right? How do you like Rhodes? Beautiful, isn't it? I've almost lost count of all the different places I've seen in the past few weeks since I arrived in Europe. Paris was the most beautiful city in my opinion, but the service in France isn't as efficient as it is in England—I had to wait hours to get a new passport when my old one got damaged. I guess they'd have been quicker about it in London. And I've seen Rome and the Colosseum, and the ruins of Pompeii. We Americans just don't have the history you Europeans do. Why, even this tiny island is full of it. It's just grand—or it was until this terrible thing happened.'

Blinking slightly at the barrage of speech, Angela looked more closely and saw the man was younger than she had at first thought—indeed, he could not have been more than about thirty, although his thinning hair and fastidious manner made him seem much older. He did not look like her idea of an oil magnate.

'No, it wasn't exactly pleasant, was it?' she replied.

'What do you think happened to this fellow—what was the name? Cavell, wasn't it?'

'That will be for the police to find out, I dare say.'

'Do you think it was an accident?'

'I presume so. Why? What else could it have been?'

'I don't know, only I thought I heard you suggest there might be something suspicious about his death.'

'Not really. I was just wondering, that's all. I dare say it will turn out that he fell into the sea accidentally and drowned.'

'Yes, yes, I dare say you're right. Only…' He turned his eyes towards the distant headland and wrinkled his forehead. 'The coast is very rocky hereabouts. Why, anyone might slip on the rocks and hit his head! That seems more likely than drowning, if you ask me, since he was young and could most likely swim. But I guess they'll have a doctor examine him and we'll find out soon enough how it happened. Didn't you say he was supposed to be on his way to Athens?'

She made some vague reply, only half paying attention to the conversation, for she had just spotted Edgar down by the little harbour, talking to someone she did not recognize, a Greek, who was standing on the deck of a boat. The Greek seemed to be demonstrating the various conveniences of his craft.

Mr. Peterson, having got over his disturbance at the sight of a dead man, appeared almost thrilled about the events of the morning and was still talking non-stop.

'Who would have thought that little old John Peterson of Andersville, Indiana would be seeing London and Rome and Athens, and stumbling across a dead body!' he exclaimed. 'Why, it beggars belief!'

He continued to talk animatedly about it for some minutes then took his leave, somewhat to Angela's relief. A short while later Edgar turned up.

'You've missed all the excitement,' she said, and told him what had happened. He raised his eyebrows and whistled.

'Good Lord! So that's where he went after he floated out of the pool. Then he was a guest here, was he?'

'It seems so—although he wasn't in the best state when

we found him, so I'm not sure how Mr. Halliday recognized him. Perhaps by his clothes.'

'Not disappointed that someone else found him first, are you?'

'Why should I be disappointed?'

'I thought you were rather fond of corpses. Wasn't that why you were on the beach?' he said slyly.

'Certainly not!' replied Angela with dignity.

Of course it was not true, and she was sure his amused look was intended purely to provoke her. Before she could say anything else, Mr. Florakis came to speak to her.

'This is terrible news!' he said. 'That such a thing should happen to a guest at my hotel! Somebody must tell Professor Delisi and Dr. Schulz—and who will tell Miss Grayson?'

'Oh, good heavens!' exclaimed Angela. 'Of course, she was engaged to Cavell, wasn't she? How terrible! Poor thing. Where is she now?'

'She is most likely at the dig with the others,' replied Mr. Florakis. 'Ah, but perhaps the police will break the news when they have finished on the beach.'

He seemed relieved that the task would not fall on him.

'There goes our chance of a peaceful holiday,' observed Edgar, as Mr. Florakis bustled off. 'I suppose we'll have officialdom crawling all over the place for the rest of the day, asking questions. Let's go out until they've finished.'

'But won't they want to speak to me?' said Angela.

'I don't see why. It's not as though you found the body yourself, is it? I shouldn't worry—by the end of today I expect they'll have found out where he went into the water and proved it was an accident.'

'I expect you're right,' replied Angela.

Chapter Six

THERE WAS a fine view from where they stood, but Angela was secretly disappointed by the acropolis itself, which was not much more than three or four ruined pillars, some broken steps and half a wall. It looked better from below, she thought, standing out in sharp relief against the deep blue sky. She would not waste the effort again.

Edgar was sitting on the wall, gazing intently at a boat as it chugged out of the harbour down below. Angela went to sit next to him and they remained in companionable silence for some minutes. They were obviously not the first people to have come here recently, for there was a scattering of cigarette-ends on the ground, on which a mountain-goat was nibbling delicately. Angela watched the goat as it tired of the cigarettes and wandered off to look for something else to eat. Back at the hotel, the news was no doubt percolating through the guests of the death of Roy Cavell.

'I feel rather a coward for getting out of the way until the squalls are over,' she said at last.

'It's for the best.'

'I suppose so.'

She chewed her lip. He looked at her.

'You want to go back, don't you?'

'We-ell, perhaps. After all, I *was* the first to find him—just not on the beach. Do you think it matters that he was in the swimming-pool? I mean, do I need to tell the police? I don't want to upset Mr. Florakis. But what if that's where he drowned?'

'Is that what's worrying you? You needn't—he certainly didn't drown there. I swam up and down that part of the pool for half an hour before you did and I'd have seen him myself if he'd been there—the water's too clear to conceal a body. He was washed in by that passing boat and the current washed him straight out again.'

'Do you think so?' Angela was slightly relieved. 'Then perhaps I won't mention it.'

'Better not. If you go around telling everyone what you saw then nobody will ever use the pool again and Mr. Florakis will look at you reproachfully and send you the worst cuts of lamb.'

'Yes.' She turned her head towards the headland below which they had found the body of Roy Cavell. 'Still…'

He sighed.

'Oh, very well, then. Let's get it over with. But you can fend off the Brinkhurst.'

They arrived back at the Hotel Acropolis just as tea was being served, so there was no avoiding the aforementioned personage, who had placed herself and her charge in the most prominent spot in the dining-room, and was stopping everyone who passed by to wonder at the tragedy and add further information about the matter to her stores. She was fortunate in her endeavours that Mr. Peterson was as eager to talk about it as she was to find out about it, and when Angela and Edgar came in they found

Peterson sitting with the two Englishwomen, deep in conversation.

'Oh, Mrs. Merivale!' exclaimed Miss Brinkhurst in her carrying voice. 'Mr. Peterson tells me you were one of the people to find poor Mr. Cavell this morning. What an unspeakable tragedy!'

'Yes, it is, isn't it?' replied Angela.

To her enormous relief the waiter just then arrived at Miss Brinkhurst's table and they were able to escape onto the terrace before she could insist they sit with her.

Outside there was activity on the beach: as Angela took her seat she could see men in the distance, passing to and fro over the rocks. At last Kostis, who seemed to know everything, came to tell them that the authorities had taken Roy Cavell away, and were reporting that it was an accident, although nobody knew exactly how he had come to be in the sea off Archangel Beach when he was supposed to be in Rhodes, catching the ferry to Athens.

After tea Angela was summoned discreetly to the manager's office to speak to two very solemn Italian *carabinieri*, who asked perfunctory questions about the circumstances of that morning's discovery. Angela answered dutifully, but could only confirm what Mr. Halliday and Mr. Peterson had already said, and when they found out that she had never met Roy Cavell they seemed to lose interest—in fact, they appeared altogether keen to play down the whole incident. On reflection, Angela could not be surprised at this, since she supposed it could not be good for the reputation of Rhodes to have its visitors turning up dead all over the place.

'Have you found out exactly how he died?' she asked. 'Is it certain that he drowned?'

'We believe so,' replied one of the policemen. 'It appears that he may have hit his head on a rock, which caused him to lose consciousness. But whether he hit his head before or after he went into the water we cannot yet say for certain. It was a very sad and tragic accident.'

It seemed they knew little more than she did. When she emerged from the manager's office she found some bustle going on in the lobby, and saw that Professor Delisi had swept in and was talking urgently to Mr. Florakis, gesturing to a white-faced Esther Grayson, who had fallen into the clutches of Miss Brinkhurst, to judge by the nurse's firm and proprietary grip on her arm. It was evident the news had reached them at the dig. As they talked a taxi could be seen drawing up outside and in came Sophia Delisi, exquisitely dressed and carrying a parcel or two. Esther Grayson drew in her breath with a hiss as the other entered, and, pulling away from Miss Brinkhurst, placed herself before Sophia Delisi, who stopped.

'I hope you're happy,' she said in a low, trembling voice.

Sophia blinked.

'What do you mean?'

'This is what you wanted all along, isn't it? It's not enough for you to own every man in the place—you're not satisfied until you've destroyed them too.'

The other woman looked at her disdainfully.

'I do not know what you are talking about, but it is very rude, what you say. I have not destroyed anyone as far as I know.'

'No? What about Roy? He's dead and it's all your fault!'

Sophia stiffened, and turned to her husband, who hastened over to her.

'Is it true?'

'I am afraid so, my dear.'

'But what happened?'

'It seems he drowned.'

'He fell from the boat, you mean?'

'No, he did not get that far. He fell into the sea here.'

She stared at him in something like fear.

'Again!' she whispered.

'Yes, and it's all your fault!' burst out Esther.

Professor Delisi looked slightly nettled, and Miss Brinkhurst, who had been watching the scene avidly, came across and interjected.

'Now, you mustn't talk like that.' She turned to the professor and his wife. 'You must forgive her—she's upset.'

'Of course I'm upset! We were going to be married and she killed him!'

The last remark came out almost as a shriek, then Esther broke down in sobs.

'You had better take her away, Miss Brinkhurst,' said Professor Delisi. 'It is not good to talk wildly like this. You must try and get some sleep, my dear.'

'Come to your room, and I will give you a preparation that will make you feel calmer,' agreed the nurse.

'I won't take it!'

Esther Grayson was eventually borne away, weeping. Sophia Delisi's face wore a closed expression; it was impossible to tell what she was thinking. After a minute she went out, presumably in the direction of her room.

'You, there,' said a voice. Angela turned in surprise and saw Lady Trenoweth, sitting alone in her chair in the now-deserted lobby.

'I believe your name is Merivale. I am Lady Trenoweth. I should be glad of your help to get to my room, since as you see, my nurse has taken it upon herself to interfere in the business of others. I can walk if required,' she added. 'But the effort is great and the after-effects painful, and I do not wish to spend the whole of tomorrow in bed.'

Despite her ungracious manner Angela took pity on her.

'Of course,' she said.

She wheeled the old woman to her room on the ground floor and took her inside.

'That is very kind of you,' said Lady Trenoweth. 'You will pardon me for inconveniencing you.'

'Not at all. I suppose it couldn't be helped—Miss Grayson was very upset at the death of her fiancé.'

Lady Trenoweth gave a loud sniff.

'I imagine she was, although she was fooling herself if you ask me. As you may have divined from that little scene, the engagement was understood to have been called off after the unfortunate Mr. Cavell became entangled with that Greek Jezebel.'

'Oh,' said Angela, wondering whether she ought to pretend she had no idea to whom the old woman was referring. Before she had made up her mind Lady Trenoweth went on:

'I don't claim to know all the details, although I'm sure Amy Brinkhurst can give you chapter and verse with dates and times, but Cavell had quite obviously tired of Miss Grayson and was dallying publicly with Professor Delisi's wife.'

'Dear me! Did Professor Delisi know?'

'Who can say?' She drew herself up in her chair, and raised a wrinkled hand wearing a heavy jet ring to straighten her shawl. 'Things are not as they were when I was a girl. Wives behaved themselves and did not parade their lovers in front of anyone who cared to see. Still, you are right. I expect he did not notice. She is just one of his gewgaws, along with the ancient vases and statuettes. He collects them by the yard and sends them off to the governor's house in Rhodes for display. A most irregular proceeding—these things ought to be in a museum. Where is your husband?' she asked, with an abrupt change of subject.

For half a second Angela did not know whom she was referring to.

'I don't know,' she answered. 'I imagine he's somewhere about.'

'Probably avoiding the commotion. Very sensible of him. Men don't like scenes, do they? Still, I'd keep an eye on him if I were you. Thank you, I have no further need of your services. I expect Miss Brinkhurst will be back soon once she has forced a dose of sedative down that unfortunate girl.'

She made a motion of dismissal and Angela took the hint and left. Back in the lobby she bumped into Professor Delisi, who was just emerging from the manager's office, having presumably been talking to the two policemen. He gave her a sad smile and introduced himself.

'I understand you are the one who discovered poor Cavell,' he said.

'No, that was Mr. Halliday and Mr. Peterson. I happened upon them shortly afterwards.'

He clicked his tongue.

'Still, I am very sorry for it. It is not a nice thing for a woman to see.'

'Do you have any idea what happened?' asked Angela curiously. 'Have they discovered where exactly he went into the water?'

'They do not know any more than we do yet,' replied the professor. 'As far as I knew Cavell had gone to Rhodes. At my suggestion he was to stay at the governor's house on Monday night for the convenience of catching the ferry to

Athens early the next morning. But I have just spoken to the governor on the telephone. He says that he and his wife were attending an official dinner that night and did not arrive home until after two, so naturally when they did not see Cavell they assumed he was already in bed. They did not find out until the next morning that he had never come at all. They were a little surprised, but assumed he must have changed his plans at the last minute.'

'I see. It looks rather as though he never left St. Michael at all in that case. Poor Miss Grayson—it's obviously come as a terrible shock to her. To you too, I imagine.'

Professor Delisi shook his head.

'Something of the kind was bound to happen to him sooner or later. He was the sort who was always in the way.'

He said it carelessly, as though Cavell's death were merely one incident out of many in his day. Before Angela could ask him what he meant, he went on, 'But I am very rude, and have not yet invited you to come and see our little dig.'

'Oh!' said Angela, taken aback at the sudden change of subject.

'Yes,' he went on, warming to his theme. 'You must come and see. There is a ruined fortress built by the Knights of St. John in 1320 or so, but next to it we have found some very well preserved Hellenistic remains and quite a treasure trove of artefacts. It is likely that the fortress stands on what was a temple, or perhaps even more than one temple. You will come tomorrow, or the day after, yes?'

'Er—'

'Good.'

He gave another nod, as though her agreement were

not in doubt, then went off. Angela watched him retreat thoughtfully. What had he meant when he said that Roy Cavell was always in the way? It seemed an odd sort of thing to say. But when all was said and done it had been an odd sort of day.

Chapter Seven

Angela decided to go up to her room and rest before dinner. Edgar was not there, but she was feeling dusty after their trip to the acropolis, so she had a bath and then lay down on the bed. She had intended to read her book, but without intending to she drifted off to sleep. When she awoke, the sun was low on the horizon and casting a wide yellow beam through the window into her room. There was still plenty of time before she would have to dress for dinner, so there was no need to get up immediately. She was lying comfortably, thinking of nothing in particular, when she heard a rustling sound and turned her head to see that someone had slipped a note under the door. Rising from the bed, she went to pick it up. It had been shoved vigorously and had gone partly under the rug. She lifted the edge of the rug to pull it out and saw to her surprise a second note, which had evidently been delivered in the same way. How long had it been there?

The first note was a telephone message from Edgar, to say that he was in St. Michael and would be late, so she was not to wait for him if she was desperate for dinner. She grimaced and turned to the other one. There was no name on the envelope, and she tore it open to find a type-written message that said:

> *I have looked into the matter and everything is explained. Say nothing to anybody—it will only cause trouble. I will tell you more this evening before you go.*

IT WAS unsigned and dated two days earlier. Angela stared at it, perplexed. It could not possibly be meant for her—or for Edgar either, since they had arrived only yesterday. She regarded the note thoughtfully for a while, then dressed and went down to dinner. Mr. Florakis was at the desk.

'Who had our room before us?' asked Angela.

He glanced at the register and his face fell.

'I am afraid it was poor Mr. Cavell. I told him I should not be able to keep it for him for the week he was away, since it is one of the nicest rooms and we have other guests to think of, but he was quite understanding and did not make a fuss. Is it a problem? Perhaps you do not like the idea of staying in his room after what has happened? If you think it is bad luck there is another room, but it is not so nice.'

'No, no, that's quite all right,' Angela assured him. 'We're perfectly happy in the room, thank you. I don't suppose you know anything about a message that was delivered to Mr. Cavell two days ago? I found it pushed under the rug.'

Mr. Florakis knew nothing of any such message, although it was possible that one of his staff had delivered it. He promised to ask them about it, and Angela went in to dinner.

The dining-room was quieter than usual; there was no sign of Professor and Mrs. Delisi or Esther Grayson, who was presumably resting in her room. Angela had just taken her seat when Miss Brinkhurst came in and made a bee-line for her.

'I must thank you for taking care of my charge this afternoon,' she said. 'Naturally I would not have left Lady Trenoweth for more than a few minutes, but she is somewhat impatient, as you have discovered.' She gave a little whinny of laughter.

'That's quite all right. How is Miss Grayson?'

'Asleep, thank goodness. I was able to persuade her to take a sedative. So unfortunate that she worked herself up like that. It was a most unpleasant scene. Naturally she was upset, but to accuse Mrs. Delisi of being responsible for Mr. Cavell's death—why, I don't wonder she and the professor have decided to keep out of the way this evening!'

Her eyes positively glittered, and Angela could almost have sworn she had licked her lips.

'Of course it was nonsense,' she replied briskly, for she was finding Miss Brinkhurst's evident pleasure in others' misery distasteful and wished to quash it as far as possible. 'The police believe it was an accident.'

'I shouldn't be so sure,' said Miss Brinkhurst knowingly. 'In fact, I wonder whether it mayn't have been a deliberate act on his part. You see, I happen to know that Mr. Cavell had had a disappointment shortly before he disappeared.'

She eyed Angela, and clearly wanted her to inquire further, but Angela would not give her the satisfaction, so she lowered her voice and went on anyway:

'You may remember I told you about Mr. Cavell's fascination with Mrs. Delisi—well, what I *didn't* mention at the time was a conversation I happened to overhear between them just after tea on Monday afternoon. It was quite by chance, you understand, since I should never dream of eavesdropping. It is just that I was sitting behind a large plant and they did not see me. Besides, they did not take the trouble to keep their voices down. At any rate, Mr. Cavell asked Mrs. Delisi to leave her husband and come away with him to Athens, and she refused!'

'I see,' said Angela, who was interested but determined not to show it. Fortunately, Miss Brinkhurst was equally determined to tell her story.

'Think of that!' she went on. 'He wanted to take her back to America with him. She had obviously tired of him, however, because she refused absolutely, and even went so far as to deny that there had ever been anything between them! Which was ridiculous, because anyone with eyes in their head could have seen what was going on. And what better reason do we need to deduce that Mr. Cavell took his own life than his guilty infatuation for a woman he wanted but could never have?'

She eyed Angela triumphantly.

'I imagine the police will have taken suicide into consideration,' said Angela. 'Have they searched his luggage for a note?'

'I don't believe so. His trunk is still in the store-room— I saw it there myself not half an hour ago when I was fetching Lady Trenoweth's wheelchair.' Miss Brinkhurst stopped suddenly and frowned. 'I wonder,' she said thoughtfully.

Angela decided that she might as well try and get some useful information out of the nurse while she was here.

'When was he last seen?' she asked. 'Does anybody know?'

Miss Brinkhurst's brow cleared.

'Yannis the taxi-driver says he had been instructed to take Mr. Cavell into Rhodes at six o'clock on Monday evening, but Mr. Cavell came to him at about half past five and told him he no longer needed him. Then he went away, but Yannis doesn't know where. As far as anybody can tell, Yannis was the last to see him.'

'It sounds as though he'd decided not to go,' said Angela. 'I wonder why.'

'As a matter of fact, I did hear that he was not especially enthusiastic about going to Athens at all, and was only going because Professor Delisi sent him.'

'Perhaps he persuaded the professor to change his mind.'

'Perhaps.' Miss Brinkhurst made as if to move on, but then stopped. 'You know, it's the strangest thing, but I have been thinking ever since you arrived that I know your face from somewhere. Have we met before?'

She was staring hard at Angela with a calculating look on her face, and despite herself Angela felt a little chill of fear. She fought it down.

'No, I don't believe so,' she replied.

'And yet you look very familiar. But I dare say you're right. Perhaps I have met someone who resembles you.'

'That's more likely. Don't they say we all have a doppelganger? Perhaps you met mine,' suggested Angela.

Miss Brinkhurst gave her one last searching look and passed on, and Angela let out a breath she had not realized she was holding in.

A few minutes later Edgar joined her.

'Sorry I'm late, darling,' he said. 'I've been in St. Michael hunting for cigarettes. The tobacco on this island can only be described as unsmokeable.'

'Did you find any?'

'Nothing tolerable. I tried every shop in the place, I should think, including the butcher's, the baker's and the candlestick-maker's, but they all sold the same ones—those foul-tasting abominations in the blue packets. Apparently Italian regulations state specifically that we must all suffer inferior cigarettes for the greater good.'

'Dear me! How tiresome for you.'

'It is, rather. Anyway, I ran across the captivating Mrs. Delisi outside the book-shop, working her magic on that author fellow Halliday. I couldn't tell whether he was relieved or annoyed when I joined them.'

'The latter, I imagine.'

'Are you familiar with him? From something he said I gather he's quite well known.'

'Yes, he is—haven't you read his book, *After the Wind an Earthquake*? It was rather good, but very earnest. He has lots of things to say about the deeper meaning of life.'

'Never heard of it. I'm afraid my tastes run to the lighter sort of literature.'

'Ah yes, that collection of French novels you keep in your study and think I don't know about,' said Angela sweetly. 'I leafed through one or two of them while you were away. *Most* instructive.'

'If you found them you might at least have had the decency to send them to me at Clairvaux. Then the time might have passed a little more pleasantly.'

'I do believe you have no shame at all.'

'I expect I did once. What are they recommending this evening?'

He lost himself in perusal of the menu. Angela said:

'It seems we're in Roy Cavell's old room. I found a note under the rug that must have been for him.'

He glanced up.

'Did you?'

She brought out the note and showed it to him. He raised his eyebrows.

'What were you doing reading his letters?'

'There was no name on the envelope, so I thought it might be for me, but it must have been for Cavell as it's dated the day he left. Look.'

He read it.

'Very cryptic. I expect it's a note from his Greek seductress arranging an assignation.'

'Do you think so? It doesn't look like anything of the sort to me. Besides, it's type-written. Do lovers type notes to one another? It seems oddly formal.'

'"I refer to yours of the 3rd inst." No, I suppose not. I wonder what it is, then.'

'I don't know, but it's dated two days ago—that's the day he disappeared. "I will tell you more before you go." It must be referring to Cavell's trip to Athens. I wonder if the note has anything to do with what happened to him.'

He threw her a sceptical glance.

'Are you looking for mystery again?'

'Not at all, but you have to admit mystery seems to look for me.' She put the note away. 'I dare say it's nothing, but I'd like to be sure. A man dies and now here's a note full of cloak-and-dagger instructions not to tell anybody something—what, though? Did the person who wrote the note speak to Cavell before he went?'

'I should imagine not, since you found the note under the rug so Cavell obviously didn't receive it,' Edgar pointed out.

'True. But *somebody* wanted to speak to him before he left. As far as we know, the last person to see him was the taxi-driver, who was told his services were no longer required. But what happened between that time and the time the body was found? Why didn't Cavell go to Rhodes?

Did the mysterious correspondent find him and tell him something that caused him to decide to remain here? Nobody seems to know anything about what Cavell did in the hours before he died.'

'I think you're reading too much into it,' said Edgar.

'I beg your pardon,' came a voice, and they looked up to see Mr. Peterson, who was sitting at the next table. He leaned over and addressed Angela confidentially. 'I'm very sorry, but I couldn't help overhearing the last part of what you just said. So you do think there is something untoward about Roy Cavell's death after all!'

'I shouldn't say that exactly,' she replied. 'It's just that I've done a bit of detecting in the past and I expect it's given me an overly suspicious mind. I don't like unanswered questions, you see.'

Peterson gaped at her, then clasped his hands together in excitement.

'A fellow detective!' he exclaimed.

'No, not really. It was mostly accidental.' She noted the use of the word 'fellow'. 'Do you mean to say you...'

A look of mixed modesty and complacency crossed his face.

'Well, I shouldn't call myself a detective as such, but I have done a little bit of investigating, in a very small way, of course. I have on more than one occasion surprised an employee in the act of theft or embezzlement. It's quite a joke among my staff these days. They call me Mr. Pinkerton—just in fun, you know. I don't mean to say I'm a real sleuth, but I don't mind boasting that my powers of observation are sharper than most. I'm particularly good at reading people's characters. You, for example, Mr. Merivale. I should say by looking at you that you work or have worked in a position of great trust and responsibility

—if I were to make a guess I'd say perhaps you had an important position in a bank.'

'My word, that *is* clever!' said Edgar, as Angela turned her face away to hide a laugh. 'How could you tell?'

'I don't know, it's just a gift I have.'

'You ought to cultivate it.'

'Thank you,' said Mr. Peterson gravely, and went back to his dinner.

For the rest of the meal Edgar talked relentlessly to Angela about his work at the bank.

'You are the absolute limit,' she said, once Peterson had taken himself off.

'Well, naturally I didn't want to disappoint the fellow after he'd identified me so confidently.'

'I don't know what he was thinking—you don't look anything like a banker.'

'No? What do I look like?'

She regarded him, her head on one side.

'I'm not sure. You told me once you were a police detective and convinced me for a while, but I wonder whether I'd be convinced again if we were meeting now for the first time. At any rate, I certainly wouldn't take you for a lawyer or a factory-owner or an insurance-man or anything like that.'

'I should hope not. They all sound tremendously dull.'

'Well, you're anything but that!' she said with a laugh.

Chapter Eight

'Let's go for a walk,' said Angela after they had eaten.

'In the moonlight? How very romantic.'

'Yes. This is our honeymoon, after all.'

He regarded her quizzically but did not reply. The two Italian policemen were sitting at a table as they passed through the lounge. They seemed to have decided to make a night of it, and were keeping Kostis busy. Angela glanced at Edgar, but he appeared unconcerned at the presence of the policemen and merely returned her look with a smile.

They set off from the hotel and began walking in silence along the road that ran parallel to the cliff top in the direction of Rhodes. Angela seemed to have a purpose in mind.

'Very bright, this moon,' Edgar remarked after a little while.

'Yes.'

'A rather convenient light to see by if one happened to be looking for something.'

She did not reply.

'Don't think I don't know what you're doing,' he said.

'You don't mind, do you? After all, he must have gone in somewhere, and it struck me when I was down on the beach that this was the most likely place—that is, where the road runs close to the edge of the cliff. This stretch here is really the only place where one can come near it: one would have to scramble over a lot of scrub everywhere else to get to it.'

'He might have gone in anywhere—by the hotel or further up the coast.'

'It doesn't seem likely. He'd practically have to have waded in deliberately to have drowned near the hotel, and why should he have gone in further up the coast when as far as everybody knew he was either here or in Rhodes? No, it must have been around here, surely. And this particular spot is the only place that has the sea directly below it rather than sand or rocks.'

'True, but I don't know what you expect to find.'

'Nor do I, but it can't hurt to look.'

They stopped at a point where the road came to within about thirty feet of the cliff edge and then curved away from it again. There was a scrubby path of sorts that led away from the road and ran parallel to the cliff top. Angela left the road and headed towards the edge of the cliff. Here the ground was rocky and sandy under foot, punctuated with tussocks of grass, dried shrubs and loose rocks.

'Careful,' said Edgar as she approached the edge. 'Don't stumble over one of those rocks. You don't want to go in too.'

'I won't.' She gazed around. In the daylight this would be a good place from which to admire the view. Eighty feet below she could hear the waves whooshing gently against the foot of the cliff.

'Do you think he fell from here?' asked Edgar, coming to stand beside her.

'It's possible.' She turned and began to scan the ground.

'It's too dark for that sort of thing,' observed Edgar. 'You ought to have waited until daylight.'

'Yes, I suppose it was a silly idea. We're unlikely to see anything even with this bright moon.' She mused. 'I wonder when he went in, exactly. We know for certain he was dead by about five on Tuesday, since that's when I saw him in the pool. But there's a good twenty-four hours between then and when he was last seen on Monday. He was due to stay at the governor's house in Rhodes that night and then catch the ferry early on Tuesday. He never turned up, but he must have been intending to, since if he'd changed his mind he would surely have sent a message to the governor to tell him not to expect him, don't you think?'

'Yes. And that suggests he died some time on Monday evening for the same reason.'

'It does, doesn't it? Let's say it happened between about 5.30 p.m. on Monday, when he dismissed Yannis, and 2 a.m. on Tuesday, which is when the governor arrived home —although I expect he was dead even before that. At any rate, I think it's safe to assume he never went to Rhodes at all.'

Edgar went closer to the edge of the cliff and glanced over thoughtfully, then turned to retreat. As he did so his attention was caught by something in a patch of scrub. He stooped to pick it up.

'What is it?' said Angela.

He held it out. It was a tiny scrap of paper. She took it and held it so that the moonlight shone on it. It seemed to have been torn from a letter written on a sheet of headed note-paper. She peered at it, then gave up.

'Your eyes work better in the dark than mine do. What do those printed letters say?'

'S-A-,' he read. 'And that looks like part of a V. This is from the Savoy, if I'm not much mistaken.'

'The Savoy! How odd. Do you think it belonged to Cavell?'

'I doubt it has anything to do with him. Why, it might have been here weeks!'

'Oh, I don't think so. The paper is quite dry and hardly weathered at all.' She stared at the scrap of paper. 'Did he tear it deliberately? I wonder what it said. What does it all mean?'

'I don't suppose it means much at all. The letter might be anybody's, and even if Cavell did come along here I expect he merely came out for a stroll, lost his footing and fell in.'

'You're probably right.'

A faint light bobbed up and down out to sea, and the sound of a boat engine drifted across the water towards them —presumably a night-fisherman bringing in his catch. Angela turned away and looked back the way they had come.

'There's somebody up at the acropolis,' she said. 'Look, can you see the light? I wonder what they're doing up there at this time of night.'

'Enjoying the moonlight like us, I expect,' replied Edgar. 'But there's not much to do out here. Let's forget Cavell for now and go back to the hotel. He won't be any more dead for it, and we can have a drink.'

'It really is a very convenient place to fall in,' she said, glancing back at the edge of the cliff.

'Or to do this.'

He slid his arms around her, but she shook her head in warning and pulled away.

'Beautiful evening, isn't it?' she called, as Edgar raised his eyes to heaven at the sight of Mr. Peterson, who was toiling along the path towards them. He hailed them cheerily.

'I see we had the same idea,' he said. 'All this talk of detective-work just put poor Cavell in my mind. What have you found?'

'Nothing much, just a scrap of paper,' replied Angela. 'I don't know what it is.'

She did not mention that they had identified it as having come from the Savoy. Mr. Peterson was quite welcome to identify it for himself. Peterson took it and looked at it with a frown.

'Can't tell much from that. I wonder, now...'

They watched as he began walking to and fro, peering closely at the ground as he went. Every so often he let out an exclamation and bent to examine something. He poked at the bushes, then spent several minutes staring at an unusually-shaped rock, his head on one side.

'Hmm,' he said eventually. 'Not much to see here.'

'It's dark,' pointed out Edgar.

'True.'

At last he seemed to come to a conclusion.

'I have a theory,' he announced importantly. 'I believe Roy Cavell's death was not an accident. Yes,' he went on as Angela regarded him in surprise, 'I'm certain that what we have here is a case of suicide. Cavell killed himself, and I can prove it.'

'How?' asked Angela.

'If you don't mind I'll keep *that* to myself until I've confirmed what I need to find out. We can compare notes later if you like.'

He tapped his nose and bustled off back in the direction of the Hotel Acropolis.

'You didn't tell him where the torn paper came from. Don't want him to take any credit, is that it?' Edgar said slyly.

'I don't know what you mean,' replied Angela with dignity. 'I didn't think it was important, that's all.'

'Well, he obviously believes he's solved the mystery, so it seems you have a rival,' he said.

––––––––

THE HOTEL WAS quiet when they arrived back, most of the guests having presumably retired for the night. Only the two policemen remained sitting in the lounge, clearly in no mood to stop drinking just yet. As Angela and Edgar entered, Kostis was just coming in, looking slightly harassed and out of breath. He confided to them that the policemen had kept him run off his feet, and that he had only with some persuasion managed to get permission from Mr. Florakis to run quickly into the village and see to his sick father, who would not have eaten otherwise.

'Isn't there someone else who could look after him?' asked Angela.

'Only my brother Yannis, but he is out fishing tonight. Ah, there they are again,' he said, as one of the *carabinieri* rose and tottered across to the bar, looking very much the worse for wear. He banged on the bar and called loudly for service. Kostis made a face of comical resignation and went to answer the call, while Angela and Edgar retired to their own quarters, Angela feeling as though it had been a long day.

––––––––

Much later Angela awoke with a start. For a moment she wondered why, until she saw that the full moon was sinking in the sky and sending a beam of bright light through a gap in the curtains and directly into her eyes. She rose silently with the intention of drawing the curtains properly closed, and immediately saw that Edgar was not there. Her watch said twenty past two. What was he doing out of bed at this time of night? He was a nocturnal creature by habit; had he been unable to sleep and decided to go for a walk? It seemed a strange sort of thing to do, but there was no accounting for other people's whims. She ignored the sudden knot in her stomach and looked out of the window, but it was too dark to see anything except a light out to sea. Perhaps it was Yannis, still out fishing in his boat.

She returned to bed and lay awake, waiting for Edgar to return, and in the meantime pondered the question of Roy Cavell and his puzzling death. Mr. Peterson believed it was suicide, but Angela was not so sure. Cavell *might* have killed himself, since he had just been rejected by Sophia Delisi, but there were one or two other little circumstances that needed explaining. What was the significance of the note under the door? Why had Cavell told Yannis he no longer required his services? That seemed to indicate that he had had no intention of catching the ferry to Athens, but why? And why had Professor Delisi claimed Cavell was always in the way? Had he been referring to Cavell's having fallen in love with Mrs. Delisi? That led Angela's train of thought to Esther Grayson, who had been engaged to Cavell. Was she lying awake tonight too, mourning her lost love? Of course, from Esther's point of view it was Sophia who had been in the way, but it was not Sophia who was dead.

At that moment an image darted into Angela's head of

Sophia Delisi, and her reaction to the discovery that Roy Cavell had died. She could clearly picture Sophia's white face as she gazed at her husband. 'Again!' she had exclaimed. What had she meant by that? Had somebody else died before Cavell? Who? Angela turned the matter over in her mind but could make no sense of it.

It was a quarter past three when Edgar returned.

'Oh, you're awake, are you?' he said easily. 'I hope you haven't been waiting for me. I thought I'd left my pocket-book in the dining-room and went down to look for it. I found it eventually between the cushions on the sofa in the lounge. Those two *carabinieri* are still there and I got talking to them, although they're well and truly sozzled so I didn't get much sense out of them.'

He slipped into bed and was soon asleep, unlike Angela, who lay awake long into the night, trying to fight off the disquieting thoughts that danced mockingly through her mind.

Chapter Nine

EDGAR SLEPT LATE the next morning, so Angela went down to breakfast alone. When she entered the dining-room she saw Sophia Delisi sitting at a table by herself.

'Do you mind if I join you?' she said. 'It seems we're both without husbands this morning and I hate eating on my own.'

'Certainly,' replied Mrs. Delisi.

Kostis arrived, looking very tired, and served coffee. Angela waited until he was gone, then decided to take a direct approach.

'What do you think happened to Roy Cavell?' she asked bluntly.

'I knew you would want to speak about Roy,' replied Sophia. 'Everyone is looking at me and thinking bad things. Still, better you than Miss Brinkhurst.'

'What bad things are people thinking?'

'They think I drove him to commit suicide. I know they think this because I have thought about it myself. I thought about it for a long time last night, wondering whether it was true.'

'And what did you conclude?'

Sophia shook her head.

'Roy did not kill himself—or at least, he did not kill himself because of me. He had the—what do you say—the rage, the caprice for me, but it would not have lasted. He was not the sort to die for a woman. He was persistent, but he was not in despair the last time I saw him. I told him to go to Athens and he said he would go and then come back and try and persuade me again.'

'Persuade you? Do you mean he wanted you to leave your husband?'

'Yes. He wanted me to go with him to America. He said he had received a letter from an old college friend who was in London and wanted to offer him a job that would pay well. Of course it was impossible, and I told him so, but he said he would not give up.'

So Miss Brinkhurst had been telling the truth. In that case it did not sound as though Roy Cavell had wanted to die. On the contrary, he had been intending to continue badgering Mrs. Delisi to come away with him.

'He was in love with you,' said Angela. 'Were you in love with him?'

'No, of course not. I am a good wife. Aldo would not be happy if I fell in love with someone else.'

'But he doesn't mind if you have men friends?'

'He is always leaving me alone to go digging and work-ing, but he understands I like to have company. And it makes him proud to know that other men are envious of what he has. Where is the harm in it, as long as I do not run away with somebody else?'

'Esther Grayson didn't quite see it like that.'

'No,' she conceded. 'It would have been better if they had both gone back to America, then Roy would have forgotten me and they would have got married. He could have taken the job his rich friend offered him and they would have been very happy.'

She fixed Angela with an earnest look.

'You must not think that I do not care Roy is dead. I am very sorry about it, but in answer to your question, I cannot be sure what happened to him. I only know it was not suicide.'

'Why did you say "Again" when your husband broke the news to you?' asked Angela.

'What?'

'When the professor told you that Roy had drowned, you looked shocked, and said "Again." I just wondered what you meant, that's all. Do you know somebody else who drowned?'

Mrs. Delisi seemed to be turning something over in her mind.

'My husband,' she answered at last.

'I beg your pardon?' said Angela in surprise.

'I was married before,' explained Sophia. 'He also drowned.' She shook the crumbs from her napkin and prepared to rise. 'But I did not love him any more, so I was not very sad. Goodbye.'

Mrs. Delisi stood up and went out, leaving Angela nonplussed at her matter-of-factness.

She finished her breakfast and left the dining-room. In the lobby she was waylaid by Mr. Peterson, who took her to one side with much winking and ostentatious placing of a finger over his lips. He was looking very puffed-up and pleased with himself.

'You remember last night I told you about my theory that Cavell killed himself?' he said. 'Well, I believe I have proof!'

'Indeed? What have you found?'

Peterson puffed up even more, if that were possible.

'You know, I suppose, that he'd fallen madly in love with Mrs. Delisi—Miss Brinkhurst put me wise to all that, and I won't deny she's a beautiful lady—Mrs. Delisi, I mean—so I can't say that I blame him. Well, I don't exactly know how it was, but I got to thinking about Cavell, and trying to put myself in his position. The word was she'd turned him down flat, and he was feeling mighty grieved about it. Could that have sent him crazy, I asked myself. He never left a note or anything like that, so I thought we'd never know. But then it occurred to me there was one thing that had been neglected, and that was Cavell's luggage. It was a long shot, but I thought there might be some clue in it as to his state of mind—perhaps a journal or something of the kind. Mr. Florakis took a little persuading, but he gave way when I pointed out the reputation of his hotel was at stake, and let me look through the trunk. I didn't find a journal, but I found something nearly as good.'

He paused impressively.

'What was it?' asked Angela despite herself.

'His passport!' replied Peterson with some satisfaction. 'Don't you see? That proves he never meant to go to Athens at all!'

'I don't quite understand. Surely the fact that his passport was among his luggage indicates that he *did* intend to go.'

'Not at all. This trunk was one he planned to leave at the hotel while he was away. Kostis took it down on Monday morning and put it in the store-room for when he returned. Cavell was intending to take only a small case for his trip to Athens.'

'And what happened to the case? Was that in the store-room too?' asked Angela.

'No,' replied Peterson.

'Then where is it?'

He waved a hand.

'I expect it's somewhere. It's not important. The important thing is that he left his passport here, and that means he never intended to leave this place at all. The fact that he was prepared to defy the professor's wishes shows he'd ceased to care about what happened to him. I put it to you that when the lovely Mrs. Delisi refused to leave her husband, it caused a temporary insanity in Cavell's mind.' Peterson put his hand to his heart and assumed a tragic air. 'At that moment he decided he no longer wanted to live. He walked along the cliff top, distraught, I dare say thinking of his life and the years of unhappiness that stretched ahead of him without the woman he loved. Perhaps he found himself unconsciously approaching the cliff edge—then in the torment of his mind he stepped forward once, twice, three times, and at last took that final step into oblivion.'

Angela could see at least two flaws in his argument—first, if the fact that Cavell's passport had been found in his trunk proved he had not been planning to go to Athens, then why had he packed the trunk at all? It seemed far more likely that Cavell had merely packed the passport in the wrong case by accident. Second, where was the small case Cavell had been intending to take? Cases did not just disappear. Perhaps Peterson was right and it would turn up sooner or later, but still, it was a loose end.

Mr. Peterson was evidently waiting for congratulations on his theory, so she duly proffered them.

'Now, I don't say you wouldn't have found it out before me if you'd thought about the luggage first,' he replied magnanimously. 'We detectives have to think of everything, you know. I'm going to walk along the cliff again this morning to look for traces. If there's anything there, it'll be easier to spot in the daylight. You can tag along if you like and watch me work.'

Angela declined graciously, feeling very glad Edgar was not there to hear the conversation, since he would certainly have teased her unmercifully about it.

Mr. Peterson bustled off. Angela wanted to speak to Kostis about the trunk, but he was busy serving breakfast so it would have to wait until later. She turned and saw Edgar just coming down. He seemed in good spirits.

'Come and have a second breakfast,' he said.

'One was enough, thank you. I managed to get some marmalade on my sleeve.'

'All right then, go up and change, then we'll go down to the harbour and look at the fishing-boats.'

Angela returned to her room to survey the damage to her sleeve and mournfully wish for Marthe, her maid, who was an expert in removing sticky marks. She changed and returned downstairs, then since Edgar had not yet finished breakfast she went into the reading-room to look for a newspaper. There she found Miss Brinkhurst, who brightened when she saw Angela.

'Is it the *Times* you want?' the nurse asked, indicating a scattered pile of newspapers lying on a table next to her chair. 'Or perhaps you prefer the *Clarion* or the *Herald.*'

'The *Times*,' replied Angela, who would have died rather than admit to Miss Brinkhurst that she read the *Clarion*.

Miss Brinkhurst gazed at her copy of the *Herald* with resignation.

'Sadly out of date, these newspapers,' she said. 'It's barely worth reading them at all. I'd been following the Duke of Irmston's divorce before we left England. You know the groom was cited in the proceedings, although the Duchess denied it strongly. I expect it's all over and done with by now. And then there's the McKirdy case—that's the man who was found dead in his hotel room—and the Dexters, who posed as a butler and a housekeeper in order to steal money from their employer, and then disappeared. I expect the police have made arrests in both cases by now, but since these papers are from weeks ago we won't find out about it until after everyone else, and by that time they'll all be talking about some other story.'

'I suppose you're right,' replied Angela, taking up the *Times*.

'The *Times* is too high-brow for me,' went on Miss Brinkhurst. 'I'm not the intellectual sort at all, you see, so I'm afraid I follow the stories in papers like the *Clarion* and the *Herald* with great interest. Some people sniff and call them sensational but I adore them myself.'

She was regarding Angela with a meaningful stare. Angela began to feel uneasy.

'I see,' she said.

The nurse did not take her eyes off Angela, and her look was a mixture of slyness and triumph. Angela's uneasiness increased. Miss Brinkhurst put down her paper, rose and came to stand a little too close to Angela, who took a step back involuntarily.

'I knew I recognized you from somewhere,' said Miss Brinkhurst quietly. 'I've been racking my brains since I first set eyes on you, and this morning it came to me. You're Angela Marchmont, who was tried for murder, aren't you? And if I'm not much mistaken, that man calling himself your husband is the notorious criminal who confessed to the killing and secured your release. I recognize you both from the photographs in the papers.' Her eyes fixed searchingly on Angela's face. 'I thought he was meant to be dead, but evidently he isn't. Why are you both here, pretending to be man and wife?'

There was the slightest of pauses, then Angela did a very bad thing.

'I don't know how you've got this idea into your head,' she said stiffly. 'My name is Merivale, and I'm afraid you're quite mistaken.'

Chapter Ten

As soon as the words were out of her mouth, Angela could have kicked herself. She had promised Edgar so faithfully that she would not deny him, and yet as soon as somebody had recognized her she had done the very thing she had sworn she would not do. It was one thing to be discreet about one's past, but telling a bare-faced untruth about it was quite another. She had not kept her side of the bargain. Before she could take back the words, the door opened and they were interrupted by someone who came to tell Miss Brinkhurst that Lady Trenoweth was looking for her.

'Oh, is she awake? I'll come straightaway,' said the nurse.

She left the room, darting a malicious glance at Angela as she went. Angela had a sudden wild urge to run after her and tell her the truth, but it was too late.

'Drat, drat, drat!' she said to herself furiously. 'Angela, you fool, what on earth have you done?'

Had she been prepared for the assault, she might have answered differently, but Miss Brinkhurst had caught her by surprise and bounced her into a lie. She could not in all conscience let the deception continue, but the thought of seeking the other woman out later and abasing herself before her did not appeal in the slightest. Angela glanced at the clock and grimaced. It would have to be faced, but in the meantime she was supposed to be meeting Edgar down by the harbour.

'Why did you bring the *Times*?' asked Edgar when she arrived.

Angela looked down and realized she was still holding the newspaper.

'Oh, how silly of me! I meant to leave it in the reading-room.'

'Well, they'll just have to do without it. Let's walk.'

It was a splendid day, sunny and breezy, with clouds scudding across the sky. A stocky young man tinkering with his boat said something in Greek to Edgar as they passed, then said 'Good morning,' in English to Angela. She glanced at him and saw it was the same man with whom she had seen Edgar talking here the day before.

'Morning, Yannis,' said Edgar. 'Fine day, isn't it? Catch anything last night?'

'More than I expected,' replied the young man. Angela looked at him with interest. This, then, was Kostis's brother, the taxi-driver and night-fisherman. She wondered when he slept. As far as anybody knew, Yannis was the last person to have seen Roy Cavell alive. She wanted to ask him about it, and was just wondering how to introduce the subject when she saw him stiffen slightly and mutter something. Edgar glanced casually behind him and Angela followed his gaze to see two Italian officials approaching them. They were wearing different uniforms from the two *carabinieri* of the night before, who, Angela assumed, were still sleeping it off.

Edgar and Yannis had a brief conversation which she could not understand, although she did make out a word that sounded like '*Finanza*'. Then Edgar turned and greeted the two policemen cheerily. An exchange followed in a mixture of Greek and Italian, which Angela was unable to follow. Edgar gestured towards Yannis and then out to sea, then turned to her.

'Come on then, darling,' he said. 'Mind your step as you hop aboard.'

Before she could protest he took her hand and helped her onto the boat. Yannis was already starting the engine and casting off the rope.

'*Buon viaggio*,' said one of the Italians to her with a smile. 'You will like Lindos very much.'

'Oh! Er—I'm sure I will,' she replied, startled, as the boat bobbed and pulled away from the dock, leaving a churning wake behind it. The policemen grew smaller and smaller as they retreated into the distance, and Angela turned an inquiring gaze upon Edgar.

'I thought I'd surprise you,' he said. 'You wanted to go to Lindos, didn't you?'

'Yes, but—'

'Well then, what better day to do it? It's sunny, but not too hot with this breeze. We'll go and look around the fortress, then Yannis says he knows a taverna with wonderful views of the harbour where they do the most delicious *kakavia*.'

Angela was not fooled in the least, but she suspected the conversation would become more personal than she liked if she demanded an explanation in the presence of Yannis, so she swallowed her questions for the moment. After all, she *had* wanted to go to Lindos.

They struck out to sea until the land was almost out of sight, then turned to the South-West and followed the coast. It was very pleasant, and Angela would have enjoyed it had she not had other things on her mind. At last, after Edgar had laughingly called attention to her absent-mindedness once or twice, she felt the need to make an effort, so she did what she did best: shut her troubles firmly out of her head and turned her thoughts to her surroundings. The boat was not a new one, but it had been kept in good condition, and bore fresh blue and white paint-work. While Edgar and Yannis were talking, Angela peeped down into the cabin and spied a stack of boxes bearing labels in Turkish, several coils of rope, an old blanket exuding an unmistakable smell of rotten fish, and a crate containing some packing materials. It was much pleasanter on deck, so she went back up.

Soon they came in sight of Lindos, and as the boat nosed into the harbour Angela looked up and admired the fortress with its tall, crenellated walls, looming spectacularly above them. The rest of the morning was spent in exploring the ruins in company with a very earnest guide, who was at pains to point out the traces of each different era. The mediaeval castle of the Knights of St. John was built on older Byzantine fortifications, which in turn were built on even older foundations going all the way back to antiquity, he said, although he was dismissive of the more ancient relics as merely pagan.

After spending the morning treading over the traces of thousands of years of civilization, Angela was glad to return to the present and stop for refreshment at the taverna Yannis had recommended, where they made sure to be given the table with the best view. Angela gazed down at the harbour. The little blue and white boat was no longer there. Presumably Yannis had taken it off for a spin.

'What did those policemen want?' she asked, deliberately keeping her tone as light and casual as possible. 'You and Yannis seemed awfully keen to get away from them.'

Edgar laughed.

'Yes, we did make tracks in a bit of a hurry, didn't we? They're the Italian finance police, and they're forever snooping around and making the local Greeks' lives difficult, looking for evidence of unpaid taxes and the like. Yannis has had a brush with them before and they threatened to confiscate his boat, so he hates them. He can't trust himself not to lose his temper, so he keeps away from them as much as possible.' He made a rueful face. 'Besides, I have an instinctive aversion to the police myself, as you know. Old habits die hard I'm afraid, so my first thought when they turned up was to do a bunk. You'll forgive me, won't you, darling? I expect I'll get over my jumpiness one day.'

It sounded convincing enough, but then he was always very convincing. Angela decided to let it drop. After all, it might be the truth.

After lunch they wandered around the town, admiring the pretty houses, which Angela would have described as charmingly decayed, then they paid a visit to a shop or two, after which they made their way back down to the harbour. Yannis and the boat had reappeared, and were waiting for them. On the way back to St. Michael Angela could not help looking into the cabin again, and saw that the boxes she had noticed earlier were gone.

———

THEY ARRIVED BACK at the Hotel Acropolis during the short period of quiet between tea and dinner. Angela wanted to ask Kostis about Roy Cavell's luggage, so went in search of him.

'Yes, that is right,' he said in answer to her question. 'Mr. Florakis told me to fetch Mr. Cavell's trunk from the store this morning because Mr. Peterson wanted to look through it for clues. I do not know why it is the job of Mr. Peterson and not the police to find out what happened to Mr. Cavell, but then I remember those two stupid *carabinieri* who were here drinking until three this morning, and say to myself that there is no use in relying on them to discover anything even if it is in front of their faces. I think the police had already searched through the trunk, though.'

'Oh? Why do you think that?'

'Because they did not close it properly, and it fell open when I brought it out. I had to pick all his things up from the floor.'

'Perhaps it was Mr. Cavell who didn't fasten it properly,' suggested Angela.

'No, it was not Mr. Cavell. I brought the trunk down myself on the morning he left, and it was closed fast then.'

'A faulty catch, then.'

'That may be,' he conceded.

'I understand Mr. Peterson found Mr. Cavell's passport in the trunk,' pursued Angela.

Kostis nodded.

'Yes, and there was a note of introduction from the professor that he was supposed to give the governor in Rhodes.'

'Mr. Peterson thinks that means Mr. Cavell never intended to leave St. Michael at all, and planned to kill himself.'

'It is possible,' said Kostis doubtfully. 'But why should he kill himself?'

'Because of Mrs. Delisi.'

Kostis's face darkened.

'She is bad luck, that one. There is a scent of death around her. They say every man who goes near her dies.'

'Professor Delisi seems to have survived so far,' observed Angela.

'Perhaps. But I will be careful. Since she has been here I have carried basil in my pocket to protect against the evil eye.'

Angela suddenly remembered what Philip Halliday had said after they had discovered Cavell's body, about someone being bad luck. Presumably he had been referring to Mrs. Delisi. Poor Sophia, she thought, to be the subject of such superstition. She said aloud:

'I heard Mr. Cavell asked her to leave her husband and she refused.'

'Yes. Miss Brinkhurst was talking about it to everybody. She overheard them in the lounge.'

Angela was thinking. The facts as she had heard them did not tally. Cavell and Mrs. Delisi had not spoken until the afternoon, but Kostis had brought down the trunk in the morning. If Cavell had deliberately left his passport, having decided not to go to Athens, then it was certainly not because of Sophia Delisi.

'Do you happen to know whether Mr. Cavell had another case?' she asked.

'Yes,' replied Kostis. 'When I went in to take the trunk he was putting things in a small valise to take to Athens.'

'And where is that valise?'

'I don't know. I did not bring it down.'

'Might somebody else have brought it down?'

'I do not know who, unless it was Mr. Cavell himself. I never saw it in the store-room.'

'What did it look like?'

Kostis shrugged.

'Brown. Leather. Like any other suitcase.'

There was no more to be learned from him so she thanked him and went to find Mr. Florakis.

'Did the police search Mr. Cavell's trunk before Mr. Peterson?' she wanted to know.

No, the hotel manager informed her, the police had not asked to see it as they had been more interested in availing themselves of the hotel's well-stocked bar. And he himself had been far too upset and flustered by the events of the day to think of it.

Angela was thinking. Mr. Peterson's theory was nonsense, at any rate. If Roy Cavell *had* committed suicide then the presence of his passport in the trunk he had intended to leave behind was no indication of it, since he had packed the trunk several hours before his conversation with Mrs. Delisi. Besides, according to Sophia herself, Cavell had told her expressly that he intended to go to Athens. It appeared far more likely to Angela that he had packed the passport in the wrong place by mistake. So now they were back where they started—except that there was a missing suitcase to find.

'I wonder,' she said tentatively. 'Would you mind if I had a look at the trunk?'

Mr. Florakis was inclined to object, but Angela, following the example of Mr. Peterson, hinted that it might be for the good of his hotel to keep the matter out of police hands as far as possible, and at length he agreed.

Cavell's belongings looked as though they had been shoved into the trunk in a hurry. Angela at first thought he must have been a disorderly sort of man until she remembered what Kostis had said about the trunk falling open when he brought it out for Mr. Peterson. She looked through, but saw little of interest. There were a few letters and personal papers, but nothing that seemed to pertain to the matter at hand—and certainly nothing to show he might have intended to kill himself. One or two letters from his bank indicated that his financial position, if not substantial, was in no way precarious. There appeared to be no motive there. She frowned as something flitted across her mind. Looking through the papers again she shook her head thoughtfully.

She fastened the trunk and tested the catches. They were stiff, and difficult to open and close. There seemed nothing more to learn here, so she thanked Mr. Florakis, who had been hovering over her anxiously, and was just preparing to leave when she suddenly remembered something.

'Did you ever find out whether any of your staff had pushed a note under Roy Cavell's door recently?' she asked.

Mr. Florakis had not been able to find anyone who could recall—or would admit to—having done such a thing. Angela came away, thinking about the luggage. Kostis had said the trunk was fastened properly when he brought it down, and she had seen for herself that it could not have come loose by itself as the catches were far too stiff. But it had fallen open, which seemed to indicate that somebody had been at the luggage before Mr. Peterson. But who, and why?

Chapter Eleven

THAT EVENING they went into St. Michael for dinner, and Angela put Miss Brinkhurst out of her head as a problem to face another day. Edgar was at his most charming and attentive, and they had a very pleasant time. The island really was a delightful place for a honeymoon, dead bodies notwithstanding. They returned to the Hotel Acropolis late to find the lounge empty apart from Professor Delisi and Dr. Schulz, who were indulging in a *digestif* before bed. The professor called them across and invited them to visit the dig the next day.

'We have begun to excavate the North corner of the site this week, and have already discovered several stat-uettes and a number of pots that are almost completely intact,' he said. 'They are very fine—you must come and see them.'

They had just spent a whole day looking at antiquities, and Angela was not sure she wanted to spend yet another day doing the same thing, but the professor was so insistent that she agreed.

'Schulz will be happy to show you around,' said the professor.

Whether Dr. Schulz would be happy or not, he evidently had no choice in the matter, for Professor Delisi was a man whose authority was not to be questioned. Nevertheless, he was quick to echo the professor's assurances.

'I will make sure that everything is in good order for your visit,' he said. 'We are a little short-handed because of poor Cavell, but Miss Grayson is doing her best to make up for it. She is not exactly an expert, but then nor was Cavell.'

'No? Wasn't he an archaeologist?'

'I found him in Florence, where his uncle is the American consul and a friend of mine,' explained Professor Delisi. 'He came to me and told me Cavell had been dabbling in archaeology for a few years to the despair of his family, who wanted him to get a proper job and settle down in America. The uncle said he wanted to let Cavell —how do you say—get it out of his system, then sooner or later he would tire of it and come home. So I took Cavell to work for me as a favour to my friend. He was enthusiastic, in the way of Americans.' He threw her an ironic glance. 'He was *very* keen on writing everything down.'

'Aren't archaeologists supposed to do that?' said Angela.

'Naturally we keep records,' agreed the professor. 'But it does not make for quick progress. You will come, yes? It is not far—not more than three miles. Mr. Halliday and Mr. Peterson are coming too. Yannis will bring you all. Come at ten, and we will show you all the beautiful things.'

They agreed, then Dr. Schulz gave a great yawn, glanced at the clock and excused himself. Angela and Edgar followed his example and retired to bed.

The next morning, as they were waiting for Yannis to come and take them to the dig, Mr. Peterson took Angela aside and told her with much quiet fanfare that he had spent several hours the previous day scouring the path along the cliff top, and was certain he had found the spot where Roy Cavell went into the ocean, close to where they had met the other night.

'There were definite traces of a disturbance,' he said eagerly. 'I found a number of broken twigs on a bush close to the edge, and the ground was unmistakably scraped. I had Mr. Florakis call the police and showed them the place. They were interested, but seemed to think it bore out their assumption that it was an accident. I told them my theory of suicide but they were disinclined to accept it. They told me there was no proof!'

'There isn't, though, is there?' Angela said. 'There's no real evidence it was anything but accidental. Mrs. Delisi herself says Cavell told her he was still intending to go to Athens.'

He looked sceptical, but evidently did not wish to accuse Mrs. Delisi outright of lying.

'But you're forgetting the passport,' he said.

'That may well have been an oversight. I rather think the obvious answer will be the correct one: he went for a walk along the cliff top, strayed too close to the edge and fell over it.'

'But then why did he tell Yannis his services weren't required? That points to deliberate intent.'

'Perhaps he had found some other way to get to Rhodes.'

'Well, I guess that's possible,' said Peterson, although he looked doubtful. 'At any rate, the police will be no help. They gave me to understand that as far as they're concerned there are no suspicious circumstances, and they'll be writing a report to that effect.'

For a number of reasons Angela was herself convinced that Roy Cavell's death had not been an accident, but had no intention of confessing it to Peterson, since the last thing she wanted was to have the little American dogging her steps wherever she went for the next few days. She therefore did not draw attention to Cavell's missing valise, or the note under the door, or the other clues she had discovered—in particular, the scrap of headed paper they had found on the cliff top, which might or might not be connected to the case. Those she intended to keep to herself until she had resolved to her own satisfaction where they all fitted in.

The drive to the archaeological dig was a short one: as the professor had said it was only two or three miles inland, up in the hills. They all got out of the taxi, and Angela hung back, for she had just remembered she wanted to ask Yannis what Cavell had said to him exactly on Monday. But Yannis had no further information to impart than he had already given: Roy Cavell had asked to be taken to Rhodes, then at about half past five had sought Yannis out and said he no longer needed his services.

'Was there anything unusual in his manner?' Angela asked.

'Not as far as I could tell. But I did not know him so well, so if there was I would not have noticed it.'

She turned away and to her exasperation saw Peterson standing nearby, shaking his head at her indulgently.

'I've already asked him that. There's no clue to be had there,' he said, and went off.

Angela resisted the temptation to stick her tongue out at his retreating back. She was thinking about the period between just after tea, when according to Miss Brinkhurst's account Cavell had spoken to Mrs. Delisi, and half past five, when he had dismissed Yannis. It was not Sophia who had caused him to change his mind (assuming she was telling the truth about their conversation), since he had still been planning to go to Athens then. What had happened in that half-hour period, then? Had he spoken to somebody else?

The dig was situated at a ruined mediaeval fortress that perched on the side of a hill, looking out over the distant Aegean. Extending beyond it and across the brow of the hill were sunken traces of what had unmistakably once been another building. Several young men were digging carefully in one area of the foundations as Professor Delisi stood over them, snapping out directions. Standing close by was Sophia Delisi, who looked completely out of place, like a bird with exotic plumage in a rainy English garden. Angela heard something like a hiss of indrawn breath and turned to see Philip Halliday standing next to her, staring at Mrs. Delisi. He looked almost angry.

Dr. Schulz emerged from a hut and came to greet them.

'You see here the fortress was built from part of this older structure, which we believe was a temple to the goddess Athene,' he said. He indicated various points of interest and began to explain what they had found up to now. Mrs. Delisi just then spotted them and came over to greet them.

'Are you helping your husband today?' asked Angela.

She laughed.

'Not exactly. I should only get in the way if I tried.'

'Then why did you come?' asked Philip Halliday shortly.

Sophia turned her gaze on him.

'Aldo wanted me to,' she answered.

'If you can't help then you ought to stay at the hotel.'

He turned away abruptly and went across to speak to Edgar, who had gone across to inspect the dig close to and was standing, hands in his pockets, gazing down into a shallow pit. For a second Angela was taken aback at Halliday's rudeness, but then was visited by a sudden revelation as she remembered Edgar's remark about having bumped into the two of them in St. Michael the other day.

'He's in love with Sophia,' she thought, and was surprised she had not noticed it before. She regarded Halliday reflectively. He had been friendly with Cavell—or so he claimed—but had there been some secret resentment? Had Halliday been jealous enough of Cavell's friendship with Sophia to resort to murder?

Murder. It was the first time Angela had said the word, even to herself, in relation to Roy Cavell's death. She did not know for certain whether he had died at someone else's hand, but the possibility had to be faced. Had anyone hated Cavell enough to want him dead? It would have taken no more than an instant to do it—one quick shove and done—and Cavell would be out of the way forever. It sounded far-fetched, even to herself, that such a thing could happen in this quiet place, but there had been undeniable tensions between a number of the guests of the hotel. Had it manifested itself in violence?

The morning was spent in looking around the ruins of the temple. Dr. Schulz, Mrs. Delisi and Angela formed one group, while the others went off with Professor Delisi. Angela found it more fascinating than she had expected, since despite his appearance of nervousness Dr. Schulz had a more engaging manner than their guide at Lindos the previous day, and had a genuine knack for bringing the past to life. At last Sophia wandered off on some business of her own, and Angela took the opportunity to ask some questions about her, since it seemed that Mrs. Delisi stood at the centre of whatever had been going on here.

'Have you known Mrs. Delisi long?' she asked.

'Yes. I was with Professor Delisi in Salonika when they met—ach, it must be three years ago now. Can it be? It seems only yesterday.'

'I understand she was married before.'

'Yes. He was a fisherman who, while out with his boat one day, found a sunken wreck off Peraia containing many bronze statues. Professor Delisi and I were working at an excavation near his house in Salonika at that time, and he knew enough to bring them to us. It was a very valuable treasure, and it made Delisi very famous.'

Angela glanced at him, wondering whether he resented the fact that the professor had received all the acclaim, but his expression told her nothing. He went on:

'This man was a brute, and very cruel to his wife. But he drowned one night—perhaps fortunately for all. Sophia has had a hard life, the poor child.'

'Oh?'

Dr. Schulz nodded.

'After her husband died there was some money for her, which would have allowed her to live modestly. But alas, her husband's drunkard of a brother would not let her alone. He said he would marry her then stole all the money, and when he was attacked and killed by a ruffian in the street she was left with nothing. And a little time afterwards there was a man of ours at the dig in Salonika who was in love with her, but he died in an accident. It was most unfortunate.'

'Goodness me! No wonder Kostis thinks she brings bad luck,' said Angela. 'Although I imagine she would say she had suffered it rather than caused it.'

'These Greek peasants are very superstitious,' agreed Schulz. 'At any rate, it is fortunate that the professor fell in love with her and married her, or who knows what she would have had to do to survive?'

Angela did not think that Sophia Delisi would have remained long without a husband had the professor not been conveniently available, but she nodded her agreement.

Schulz turned to her seriously.

'Now it is hot and you have been walking all morning, so you must come and have something to drink. You will see we are not so primitive, and that we have plenty of supplies in the office.'

The 'office,' as it turned out, was little more than a room in a long hut containing two desks, several rickety bookshelves stacked high with books and academic journals, and a table laid out with various fragments of things brought up from the ground. To Angela's surprise Esther Grayson was there, sitting in front of a typewriter, apparently attempting to decipher some hand-written notes.

'Here is our home, where we are quite comfortable,' said Schulz. 'You see we have a stove and a row of cups that are all very clean. Will you make tea, please, Miss Grayson?'

'Certainly, doctor,' replied Esther.

'Afterwards I will show you our photographic dark-room, and the room where we keep all our treasures. Now, where are the others? We must give them tea also.'

Dr. Schulz disappeared, and Angela said to Miss Grayson:

'How are you?'

'Fine, thank you,' said Esther, although she did not look especially fine to Angela. Her face was drawn and pale, and there were dark circles under her eyes.

'Ought you to be working?'

'I must keep busy, and what else would I do?'

Her voice was high and brittle. She lit the stove and set a kettle to boil, then went back to her work.

'It's no good,' she said at last. 'I can't make these lists agree! It's no wonder Roy got so exasperated with them both.' She held up two dog-eared and much-scribbled-upon notebooks. 'The professor wrote this list and Dr. Schulz copied it and added things and crossed other things out, then copied it onto another page. There are things on this list that aren't on *this* one, and things on this list that aren't on *this* one, then there's a third list here that has four new things on it altogether. Or at least I think so, because it's almost impossible to read their handwriting. "See Catalogue 4." But which page of Catalogue 4? How am I ever supposed to type it all up? I wish Roy were here to explain it to me. He used to yell at them all the time about their record-keeping but I can't do that.'

'Is this his office too?'

'Yes—he sat over there.' She nodded her head towards the corner. 'He was very methodical, and did his best to keep the doctor and the professor in order. They're so terribly disorganized that I don't know how they ever get anything done.'

The others now arrived and tea was drunk from tin cups.

'Now I will show you the dark-room,' announced Dr. Schulz. 'Miss Grayson, will you come and assist?'

Everybody crowded dutifully out of the office, and, ushered by the doctor and the professor, shuffled down to the other end of the hut, where the dark-room was situated. Angela waited until everyone's attention was engaged, then slipped quietly along the corridor and back into the office. She had only a few seconds to do what she wanted to do. There was a sheaf of papers on Roy Cavell's desk and she flicked through them swiftly. They were mostly official letters. Angela skimmed through one from the governor about the head of a statue of Helios he was expecting to receive, then opened the drawers of the desk one by one and glanced through them.

'What are you doing?' came a voice, making her jump violently. It was Edgar, who had put his head in through the door.

'I left my hat,' she said, flapping the article in question, which she had deliberately left behind for her purpose.

He looked amused.

'In the drawer?'

To her supreme annoyance they were then joined by Mr. Peterson, who nodded when he saw her, and said:

'I see our minds work the same way. I searched through the drawers myself when we first arrived, but nothing doing, I'm afraid. Still, good thinking on your part. You're not too bad at this detecting, are you? I'm going to see the dark-room now.' He put a finger over his lips in an exaggeratedly conspiratorial fashion. 'I won't give you away.'

He went off, and Edgar said:

'If you're going to go rifling gaily through people's things you might at least do it discreetly instead of thundering about like a herd of elephants.'

Angela bit back a remark. She was not sure whether she was more irritated with him or Peterson. Instead she said:

'And *you* might at least make yourself useful. Keep an eye out.'

Quick as lightning she took a sheet of paper and inserted it into the typewriter.

'I haven't done this in years. Let's see if I remember.' She typed a few words quickly. 'No mistakes,' she said with satisfaction, as she tore the paper out, folded it and put it in her pocket.

'Look here, what the devil is this all about?'

'The note under the door, don't you remember?' she replied as they left the office. 'I thought it might have been typed here.'

'Of course it was typed here. Where else would it have come from?'

'I don't know, but there's no harm in making sure, is there?' replied Angela, slightly nettled, because of course he was right: who else would have typed a note to Roy Cavell but someone working at the dig?

The others were just coming out of the dark-room. Peterson threw her an approving look.

'Oh, I see you forgot your hat!' he said in a would-be casual manner that would not have fooled a child. Fortunately nobody else was listening.

'"The Rival Detectives,"' murmured Edgar as they emerged from the hut into the sunlight. 'Sounds like one of those lurid paper-backs one buys at the railway station, doesn't it?'

Angela did not deign to reply.

After the tour of the hut, Professor Delisi encouraged them to go off and explore by themselves, promising them that his men would be more than happy to answer any questions they might have. The little party quickly separated into smaller groups: John Peterson attached himself to Halliday, somewhat to Angela's relief, while Edgar had gone to stand close to Sophia Delisi, who was laughing at something he had just said. Angela watched as he offered Mrs. Delisi a cigarette and was briefly visited by an urge to go and insinuate herself proprietarily between them, but resisted it and wandered off by herself to explore the ruins of the mediaeval fortress, which she had to admit was more immediately interesting to her than the foundations of the ancient temple, since it was easier to picture it as it must have been in the fourteenth century.

She spent a happy interlude wandering in and out of the ruined walls, stopping to examine an arched doorway above which were carved the arms of the Grand Masters, and imagining how the fortress must have looked in the age of the Knights of St. John. The West side of the edifice had partly collapsed down the hill and some of the walls in that area were crumbling and unstable. Angela descended a flight of uneven steps which led outside the walls, and stationed herself in a sunny spot on the grassy hillside to look out over the landscape towards the sea.

She did not know what made her turn, but it was lucky that she did, for she was just in time to get out of the way in a hurry as a section of wall above her detached itself and toppled ten feet to the ground. As she leapt to avoid it she lost her footing on the steep hillside, skidded several feet, tripped and landed with a bump and a thump. She remained where she was for a moment or two until she had collected her thoughts (which were most unladylike), then rose gingerly to her feet. Nothing seemed to be broken or sprained, although she had grazed her left hand.

'What happened? Are you all right?'

She looked up. It was Philip Halliday, who was followed immediately afterwards by Professor Delisi.

'You have had an accident!' exclaimed the professor in concern.

Angela gazed at her hand and clothes ruefully.

'I'm quite all right, thank you—at least, I think I am. I lost my footing, that's all.'

'Well, we will clean you up as best we can and put a bandage on that hand, and then it will be as if it never happened,' said the little Italian.

'Here,' said Philip, holding out a hand to help her up the slope. 'We'd better get you back to the hut.'

Feeling not a little shaken, Angela agreed that perhaps she would like to sit down for a few minutes. Once inside the fortress walls she stopped and said:

'Just a moment.'

She went to examine the offending wall, which on this side was no more than five feet high. There were still one or two loose blocks of stone resting on it. She stared thoughtfully at the ground on the near side.

'The bricks in this wall are loose,' she said at last. 'I ought to have been more careful.'

Halliday and Delisi came to stand beside her and looked over the wall. The professor clicked his tongue in consternation.

'*Dio mio*! What might have happened! I will send one of the men immediately to make it safe.'

They returned to the hut, where Edgar and Sophia Delisi were standing. Edgar's eyes widened when he saw her.

'I am afraid your good lady has had a little accident,' said Professor Delisi. 'Thankfully there has been no great harm done, but we must clean her hand, which is sadly scraped.'

'The skin is hardly broken at all,' said Angela. 'I fear the biggest injury has been to my pride.'

The professor fussed over her and Miss Grayson tended to her sore hand and helped her brush down her clothes. Angela assured them that apart from a few bruises she was quite well, but they insisted she sit down for a few minutes.

Edgar, meanwhile, had been eyeing her curiously. As soon as there was nobody within earshot, he said quietly:

'You look as though you'd seen a ghost. What is it?'

'I hate to sound melodramatic,' she replied, 'but I rather think somebody has just tried to kill me.'

Chapter Twelve

EDGAR, to his credit, was concerned enough.

'Are you sure? Who?'

'I don't know—it all happened too quickly. The professor and Mr. Halliday turned up a minute afterwards, but I don't suppose that means anything. It might have been either of them, or someone else entirely.'

'But why do you think somebody did it deliberately?'

'Because I'd been standing in that place not five minutes earlier and noticed the stones that fell down. They were loose, but not precariously so. Either somebody pushed them off or there was an earthquake. And I'm pretty sure it wasn't the latter.'

'Could it have been the wind?' he suggested.

'Hardly. There's barely any breeze today. Besides, on the way back I stopped to look at the wall again. On the ground on the fortress side my footprints were still there in the dust where I'd been standing only a few minutes earlier, but there were other footprints on top of them.'

'A man's or a woman's?'

'A man's.'

'Hmm. Not Miss Grayson or Mrs. Delisi, then.'

'You were with Mrs. Delisi, weren't you?'

'Not all the time. She went off to flutter her eyelashes at Halliday for a bit, and I didn't see either of them after that. Perhaps we ought to go back to that wall and have another look.'

Angela shook her head.

'No good. Both the professor and Halliday trod on the footprints while I was trying to look at them surreptitiously and stamped them out.'

'Couldn't you have told them to stand back?'

'Not without making it obvious what I was looking at,' she replied. 'I might have thought of some bright idea to keep them away if I'd been quicker, but I was still quite shaken at the time.'

She was relieved he had not immediately dismissed her fears out of hand.

'But why should anyone want to kill you?'

'Well, unless somebody has taken an unconquerable dislike to my face—which I suppose is possible—I can only assume it's because I've been asking questions about Roy Cavell,' answered Angela.

'You really do think there was something untoward about his death, don't you?' he said.

'Yes, I'm afraid I do.'

'Do you want to tell the police?'

'Mr. Peterson has told them already. Apparently they're quite convinced it was an accident and aren't looking any further than that.'

They had no time to talk further because Yannis and his taxi just then arrived and they were called upon to say their goodbyes.

'All right, then, spit it out,' said Edgar when they got back to their hotel room. 'Don't think I hadn't noticed the cog-wheels revolving in your head the past couple of days. It's obvious you've got a bee in your bonnet, so you'd better tell me the whole story.'

'I didn't think you'd approve,' said Angela. 'We're supposed to be on honeymoon.'

'So we are. But if somebody's going around wanting to take a pop at my wife I think I ought to be made aware of it.'

Angela felt a little jolt at his words. '*My wife.*' How funny it sounded. They had got married more than eight months ago but had been separated immediately after the wedding and remained apart until only ten days ago, and this was the first time she had heard him say the words. She realized she had not quite seen it as real up to now. But here they were, and he was her husband and she was his wife.

'What are you gaping at?' he asked.

'Nothing,' she said, coming to herself. 'And anyway, I haven't kept anything from you as such. You've seen everything I have.'

It was *almost* true, since Miss Brinkhurst was not connected to the case and did not count.

'Very well, then, what makes you think Cavell's death wasn't an accident?'

'There are too many unanswered questions,' she replied.

'Such as?'

'First, why did Cavell tell Yannis he wouldn't be needed on Monday evening? Had he found some other way of getting to Rhodes for the ferry, or had he decided not to go at all? If the latter, why? And why didn't he let the governor know? He was expected at the governor's house that night but didn't turn up. You'd think he'd have had the good manners to send a message at least, if he'd changed his mind. Second, who wrote the note that was pushed under the door, and what is it referring to?'

She went across and fetched the sheet of paper she had found under the rug from her bedside drawer, then dug in her pocket and took out the sheet of type-writing from the dig, and compared the two side by side.

'I couldn't remember the exact words of the original note but I got it near enough. Look—the "t" and the "e" are both fainter than the other letters. The machine probably needs a new ribbon. As you so rightly pointed out, it was typed at the dig. But what does it mean? "*I have looked into the matter and everything is explained. Say nothing to anybody—it will only cause trouble. I will tell you more this evening before you go.*" We know Cavell didn't get the note, but did the person who wrote it catch him anyway before he went?'

Edgar took the note and looked at it.

'It might mean anything or nothing,' he observed. 'There's no particular reason to think it's suspicious.'

'No, but it's a mystery all the same. And then there's the missing suitcase. Cavell packed most of his luggage in a trunk and put it downstairs, but he also packed a small valise to take to Athens—Kostis saw it—and it's missing. It's brown leather, in case you happen to have seen it anywhere.'

'Might he have left it in here?' suggested Edgar. 'Didn't you say this was his room? Perhaps he left it and the maids didn't clean properly.'

'I didn't think of that,' she said. She looked around. 'We're using the cupboard and the drawers, so the only possible place would be under the bed.'

'Not there,' said Edgar, straightening up. 'That's no go, then. Are you sure it wasn't downstairs with the trunk?'

'Quite sure.'

'Then I expect it went into the sea with him and we'll never find it.'

'But why would he carry a suitcase along the cliff path? If he was going for a walk before departing for Rhodes surely he'd leave it at the hotel rather than hauling a week's luggage around with him. And there's another thing: someone has been searching the trunk he left behind.'

'How do you know?'

'Mr. Peterson wanted to look through Cavell's luggage, so he had Kostis bring it out and it fell open. I tried the catches a few times and they were very stiff and difficult to open and close, so they couldn't have come loose by themselves, and Kostis said it had been properly closed when he brought it downstairs on Monday. At a guess I should say that someone crept into the store-room to look through the trunk, but had to get out in a hurry and didn't have time to struggle with the catches, so didn't fasten them properly. Who was it, and what were they looking for?'

'You're sure of this?'

'As sure as I can be. And there's another thing—the letter.'

'Which letter?'

'Sophia Delisi mentioned to me that Roy Cavell had recently received a letter from a friend offering him a job. It wasn't in the trunk or in any of the drawers at the dig. Where is it?'

'In the missing suitcase, I expect. What has that to do with anything, anyway?'

'I don't know, exactly, but it does seem to give a clue as to Cavell's state of mind. He was thinking of taking a job, which doesn't give the impression that he was in any way suicidal.'

'The only people suggesting he was suicidal are Miss

Grayson and that absurd little American. Everyone else appears quite convinced it was an accident.'

'Perhaps I'm making too much of the letter, then. I dare say he threw it away or something.'

'Look here, none of these things are what you'd call conclusive evidence,' he said.

'No, but taken all together they're suggestive, don't you think?'

She sat on the edge of the bed and stared out of the window. Edgar sighed.

'It's obvious you won't be able to let it go until you've got to the bottom of it. But the question is, how are we going to go about finding the truth?'

She brightened immediately.

'We? Will you help me, then? Are you sure you don't mind?'

'Whether I mind or not is hardly the point.' There was an ironic glint in his eye. 'If I've learnt anything in a long and varied life it's never to get between a woman and what she wants. Besides, we don't want that jumped-up American busybody stealing a march on us, do we?'

Angela clapped her hands together.

'I knew you were a darling. I could just kiss you!'

'That's more like it.'

After a moment or two she extricated herself with some difficulty and glanced at the clock.

'It's nearly six. I'd like to go for a walk along the cliff top and look at the place Cavell went in before it gets dark.'

'Why?'

'Just something Mr. Peterson said that made me think.'

'I can think of better ways to pass the time, but if you insist,' he said resignedly.

Chapter Thirteen

WHEN THEY GOT to the place on the cliff path they had explored the other night, they found Esther Grayson there, looking out to sea. Something about her manner warned Angela that this was a moment to tread carefully. She threw a glance at Edgar and he hung back a little. Miss Grayson turned and saw Angela. She had obviously been crying.

'Mr. Peterson says this is where he went in,' she said. 'Look, you can see the marks where he slipped over the edge.'

'You oughtn't to have come here,' said Angela, secretly exasperated with Peterson and his insensitivity.

'I had to. I had to see for myself. They wouldn't let me see his body to say goodbye, so this is the nearest I can get.'

'I'm sorry.'

Esther sniffed and gulped.

'How can I go on without him?' She saw Angela's look of alarm. 'Oh, don't worry, I'm not going to throw myself after him. I did think about it when I came along here, but the idea of the fall, and perhaps hitting the rocks on the way down, and landing in the cold sea and being sucked under, and the water going into my lungs frightens me too much. I'm a terrible coward about that kind of thing, you see.'

'You're not a coward,' said Angela. 'It's much harder to stay and face things.'

'Do you think so? To me it seems harder to think that I won't see him again. I followed him out here, you know. We met when we were both at college, and I always liked him, but he never noticed me. After college I came out to Italy and took a job as a secretary at the consulate in Florence, and found that Roy's uncle was the American consul there. Then about a year and a half ago Roy came out to visit him and remembered me and we fell in love. Or at least I did. I've wondered since whether he didn't just ask me to marry him because we were thrown together. He was always kind, but there were signs even back then, now I think about it. I mean, if he loved me why would he have taken a job in Rhodes? He said I should stay in Florence but I insisted on following him out here. And then he met Sophia and fell for her. What man wouldn't? Oh, he denied it, but I knew he was lying. He watched her all the time and followed her around and made it perfectly obvious. And she encouraged him. She drew him in even though she didn't really want him, and then she couldn't rid herself of him, so she went to the professor and made him take care of it for her. That's what she always did when some man was bothering her—ran to the professor, even before she married him.'

'Goodness!' said Angela, startled. 'And how exactly did he—er—take care of it for her?'

'Why, he sent Roy to Athens on some trumped-up excuse. There was no real reason for him to go, but the professor said he needed Roy to take some papers to someone at the Archaeological School. He couldn't just send them in the mail—no, he wanted Roy to deliver them personally. But it was just a way to get him out of Sophia's hair. I guess they thought a week away would calm him down and make him come to his senses. He didn't want to go without her, though. Miss Brinkhurst overheard them talking in the lounge on Monday before he was due to leave, and just couldn't wait to come and tell me the news.' She said it bitterly. 'He was trying to persuade Sophia to leave her husband and come away with him. He had a friend who was rich and had written to offer him a job, you see. Bill had been trying to persuade him to come and work for him for years, but Roy had always turned him down because he was all taken up with archaeology and didn't care a hoot for the refining business. But Bill said he was going to come here and try and persuade him in person. I guess rich people are used to getting their own way.'

'Do you know what happened to the letter?' Angela could not help asking.

'The one from Bill? I have no idea. I never saw it, but I assume it's in Roy's trunk. At any rate, Sophia didn't want to go with him, and he went away, and somehow he ended up in the sea. And it was all her fault!' she burst out.

'Do you mean she drove him to kill himself?'

'Yes—maybe—I don't know. I just can't help thinking that if he hadn't been sent away he'd still be alive now.'

A tear was rolling down her cheek.

'If only I could have done something,' she said. 'I'd have stopped it somehow.'

Angela heard voices and glanced along the path to see Edgar talking to Philip Halliday, who was just returning from a walk.

'Go back to the hotel and try to get some rest,' said

Angela gently. 'You look as though you hadn't had a wink of sleep in days.'

'I haven't.'

'None the worse for your adventure at the dig, Mrs. Merivale?' called Halliday cheerfully as he approached. 'You're lucky you got off with just a scratch. The goddess Tyche was certainly looking down on you today. Hallo, Esther, don't tell me you've come here to brood. That sort of thing will do you no good at all. Are you going back to the hotel now? I'll walk with you.'

Esther was persuaded to leave, and she and Halliday went off together.

'An awful idea has just come into my mind,' said Angela to Edgar once they were out of hearing.

'Oh, what?'

'Just a second—I want to look around quickly before Mr. Peterson turns up, pats me on the head and tells me what a good girl I am. He told me about these marks and I wanted to see them for myself.'

She crouched down and examined the scratches on the ground that Miss Grayson had pointed out.

'Look at this.'

Edgar approached to see.

'He seems to have left an awful lot of traces for someone who merely overbalanced and toppled into the sea,' he observed.

'He does, doesn't he? Look at this area where the ground is scraped away. It starts a good five feet from the edge of the cliff.' She indicated a dry, scrubby bush. 'And see these snapped twigs?'

'Do you think he grabbed hold of it to try and save himself?' He regarded the bush thoughtfully, judging the distance between it and the cliff edge. 'No, that doesn't work, does it? The broken twigs are on the wrong side.'

'Besides, if he lost his balance this far back he wouldn't fall in. It looks more as though something was dragged past the bush.'

'I suppose you're going to say the something was a corpse.'

'Perhaps. Convince me it wasn't.'

'It might have been the missing suitcase.'

She considered.

'I don't think so: Kostis described it as a small valise. That wouldn't be heavy enough to make such marks. Are you suggesting he threw the suitcase over the edge and then jumped after it?'

'He might have followed it by accident. No, I know it doesn't make much sense, but it's the best I can do.'

'Well, keep thinking, but for now we'll assume the marks were made by Roy Cavell—or his dead body, at any rate, as I doubt he was conscious when it happened. At least, I hope he wasn't. The police said he hit his head before or after he went in, and I'd be happier if I could be sure it was before.'

'What was your awful idea?'

She stood up.

'Did you know Professor Delisi is Sophia Delisi's second husband?'

'No.'

'Her first was a fisherman in Salonika who by all accounts treated her very badly.' She eyed him sideways. 'He drowned.'

'Did he, now?'

'Yes. Dr. Schulz told me about it. Apparently this fellow was the one who originally found the Peraia Bronzes and brought them to Professor Delisi, which I assume is how the professor met Sophia.'

'I see.'

'Then her husband's brother wanted to marry her, but instead he stole all her money. He died too—killed by someone in the street. And after that a man working for the professor fell in love with her but died in an accident.'

'Rather a run of bad luck for her.'

'Yes—and even worse, people started saying she *was* the bad luck.'

'Hoodoo aside, you're not seriously suggesting she's been bumping off every man who offends her, are you?'

'I wasn't thinking of her, no. But what about Professor Delisi? When I was talking to Esther just now she said that Sophia has been in the habit of running to him every time a man is bothering her.'

'The professor?'

'Why not? He's an egotist and seems to think of her as a pretty possession rather than a wife. Lady Trenoweth said Sophia was a gewgaw to him, a sort of trophy, and Sophia herself told me he got a kick out of knowing other men wanted her and couldn't have her. He doesn't mind them buzzing around her but woe betide any man who gets too close. I'd very much like to know the circumstances of her husband's death—and that of his brother and the other man who wanted to marry her in Salonika.'

'You think there may be more to their deaths than meets the eye?'

'Perhaps.'

'Very well, then, let's put him down as a suspect. Who else? You really ought to consider all possibilities. I laughed at the idea of Sophia Delisi being a murderer just now, but might she have done it?'

'I can't see it somehow,' replied Angela doubtfully, after a moment's thought. 'She doesn't seem the active type. It appears to me that she's always been accustomed to having things and people come to *her*, rather than having to go after what she wants, if you see what I mean. That's why the idea of the professor sprang to mind. If she wanted Cavell out of the way she wouldn't do it herself—she'd get her husband to do it.'

'Yes—I can't really see her pushing anybody over a cliff and ruining her nails. What was the professor doing on Monday night, I wonder? It would help if we knew exactly when Cavell had died, then we could look for alibis and eliminate some people.'

'Well, unfortunately we don't, so there's nothing to be found out that way at present.'

'In a perfect world it would be the ghastly Miss Brinkhurst who'd done the deed,' said Edgar. 'Although what her motive might be I can't imagine.'

Angela did not want to be reminded about Miss Brinkhurst.

'Well, we'll leave her out of it, and Lady Trenoweth, since as you say there isn't any obvious reason for either of them to want him dead,' she said. 'I did wonder about Philip Halliday, though.'

'Halliday? Why on earth should he want to do it?'

'He's in love with Sophia Delisi.'

'I thought he hated her. I've never heard him say a good word about her.'

'But why should he dislike her so much? As far as I'm aware they hardly know each other. It's an unwilling attraction, certainly, but it's there all right. I saw it today at the dig. And if he's in love with Sophia, he might have been jealous of Roy Cavell.'

'Enough to push him into the sea? Do you have any proof?'

'Of course not—this is all pure speculation, but that's all we can do for the present. Now, who else had a motive?'

'Miss Grayson,' said Edgar.

'Oh, surely not! You saw how distraught she was just now.'

'Of course she was distraught. She was in love with him and now he's dead—but that doesn't mean she didn't shove him in. She'd been ditched for another woman and was hopping mad about it. "Hell hath no fury like a woman scorned," and all that.'

'Mad? I should have said she was more despondent than angry.'

'So you say, but we found her here just now, in exactly the place he's supposed to have died. How did she know where he went in?'

'Peterson told her.'

Edgar made an impatient noise.

'Why did he have to stir the pot? That fellow's a thorn in the side. I shouldn't be at all surprised to find out he murdered Cavell himself purely in order to stride about making himself look important. If he's not careful some-body will push him in too.'

Angela was secretly entertained that he now seemed to find Peterson as irritating as she did.

'The thought had crossed my mind,' she said. 'But I'm afraid he arrived in St. Michael the same day as we did, by which time Roy Cavell was already dead, so we must regretfully cross him off the list.'

'Well, then, assuming it wasn't Kostis or Yannis or Mr. Florakis, that leaves only Dr. Schulz. Any motive there?'

'Not as far as I can tell, unless he was tired of being badgered about his record-keeping. Apparently Cavell used to tick him off about it all the time.'

'Not the strongest reason to kill someone.'

'No.'

There was a scuffling sound just then and a mountain-goat appeared over the rim of the cliff.

'They're awfully sure-footed, aren't they?' said Angela. 'It's a pity Roy Cavell hadn't been a goat.'

The goat stared at them for a moment then wandered off along the path.

'So, then, now we come to the attempt on your life,' said Edgar. 'Who did it, and was it the same person who killed Cavell? Let's assume the answer to the second question is yes.'

'We've no reason to think it wasn't,' agreed Angela.

'Who might have done it? Neither of the women, you say, since the footprints were wrong—unless one of them changed into a handy pair of men's boots and hared along to the fortress after you.'

'That implies a high degree of premeditation, though, whereas I should have said this was a purely opportunistic attempt. After all, who could have known I would go and stand below that particular wall? I didn't even know it myself. No, whoever did it certainly didn't plan it in advance.'

'Well, then, let's look at motive. Who knew you were investigating Roy Cavell's death? Peterson, obviously. Now, what do you think about him as a suspect? He wants all the *kudos* for solving the mystery and you've been trampling all over his territory and cramping his style.'

'That would be rather petty of him, wouldn't it?'

'I should say "petty" describes him to a T.'

'Perhaps, but it also doesn't fit with our theory that the same person who made the attempt on my life also killed Roy Cavell.'

'It doesn't, no,' he agreed. 'But our theory might be wrong.'

'I should say it was far more likely that Peterson had been talking to someone else—perhaps Miss Brinkhurst. And if Miss Brinkhurst knows I've been looking into Roy's death then so does everybody, so our murderer might easily have found out about my detecting from her.'

'Yes, that makes sense. In that case it might have been any of the men who were at the dig today—the professor, Halliday or Dr. Schulz. Didn't you say Delisi and Halliday turned up at the same time?'

'Do you think it might have been a joint enterprise? Dear me! Perhaps people really do dislike my face.'

'Impossible!' he said mockingly.

She thought, trying to remember.

'No, they didn't arrive exactly together. Halliday arrived a few seconds before the professor, although he's younger and can probably run faster. How can we find out where they both were when it happened without accusing either of them of attempted murder?'

'"I hope you don't mind my asking, but did you push a pile of rocks onto my head?" No, not the best approach, is it? Then I suggest we ask them something nicely vague about whether they saw it happen.' He looked at her. 'What is it?'

'I'm wondering whether we oughtn't to tell the police about our suspicions.'

'Didn't you say Peterson's already done that?'

'Yes, but he was trying to convince them it was suicide, not murder.'

'Try if you like,' he said. 'They might be more inclined to listen if two of you are trying to persuade them it wasn't an accident—especially two foreign tourists. By the way, you will be careful, won't you? If it's true that someone's trying to get you out of the way they might try again. Don't go too near any cliff edges.'

She had been gazing over the cliff, but involuntarily took a step back.

'Don't worry, I'll keep an eye out,' she said.

He smiled.

'Good. I'm tired of losing wives all over the place. I'd like to keep this one for a while.'

'You talk as though you lost a wife every week.'

'Well, once was quite enough.'

There it was again. '*My wife*'. She felt another twinge of guilt at having lied to Miss Brinkhurst, and resolved to go and find the nurse as soon as they got back to the hotel, in order to set the record straight.

Chapter Fourteen

AS SHE DRESSED FOR DINNER, Angela arranged in her head what she should say to Miss Brinkhurst. She intended to take the woman into a private corner, admit to her real name splendidly and without shame, then turn on her heels, stalk away and take her place proudly beside her husband. She even felt some sense of pleasurable anticipation at the idea of standing up and doing the right thing. Let people say and think what they liked: she had married the man she loved and would not slink about like a rat apologizing for it.

To her enormous vexation, however, when they entered the dining-room neither Miss Brinkhurst nor Lady Trenoweth was anywhere to be seen. Having fortified herself against a confrontation, Angela felt oddly cheated, and went to inquire at the desk, but was informed that the two ladies had gone out to dinner. Angela waited impatiently for them to return. At eleven o'clock she inquired again only to be told they had come back an hour ago and retired to their rooms. Angela toyed with the thought of marching to Miss Brinkhurst's room and hauling her out of bed, but rejected the idea as being unlikely to advance her purpose. But the ladies were not at breakfast the next morning either, and she found out from a passing remark by Miss Grayson that they had gone into Rhodes for the day. There was nothing to be done, so Angela swallowed her frustration and tried to put it out of her mind.

The Delisis were sitting at the next table. Professor Delisi made a point of inquiring after her health and was pleased to find she had come to no harm.

'And what are you doing today?' he asked.

'We thought of going into Rhodes,' replied Angela. 'We've been here since Tuesday, and it's Saturday now and we still haven't seen it properly.'

'You will like it very much,' said Mrs. Delisi. 'There are shops and places to eat and lots of nice people.'

'Poor Sophia,' said her husband indulgently. 'You do not often get the chance to go to Rhodes and show off your beauty to the world. Still, we will go there dancing tonight and you will be very happy.'

'Will you come?' Sophia asked, addressing Angela and Edgar. 'It is at the Grand Hotel in Rhodes. They have dancing every Saturday and there will be many people there.'

'I haven't been dancing in a long while,' said Angela. She looked at her husband. 'Shall we go?'

'Why not?' he replied, and so it was agreed.

They spent the day in the old town, taking in the mediaeval palaces, mosques and minarets, but Angela found it difficult to concentrate or enjoy it as much as she ought, since she could not help looking out for Miss Brinkhurst and Lady Trenoweth, who were also in Rhodes today. Wherever they went she turned her head this way and that, looking for the familiar sight of the wheelchair, its occupant and her companion, but if they were in Rhodes she saw no sign of them.

They went back to their hotel to rest and dress for dinner. The first person Angela saw as they entered was Lady Trenoweth, who seemed to be haranguing the man behind the desk about something. She was without her wheelchair, leaning heavily on a stick.

'This is not to be countenanced,' Angela heard her saying. 'I did not hire a nurse only to have her wander off whenever the mood takes her. I am tired after our trip today and require attention that only she can provide. I should be obliged if you would send her along to my room post-haste as soon as she returns.'

She turned away discontentedly as the man behind the desk shrugged. It looked as though Miss Brinkhurst had gone out somewhere, so Angela's confession would have to wait another day.

In the evening they returned to Rhodes for the dance at the Grand Hotel, which was a much bigger and livelier place than the Hotel Acropolis. Having led a fairly retired life since Edgar's arrest Angela had forgotten how much she enjoyed dancing and company. They danced a little, drank a little, lost a little at the casino and altogether had a most agreeable time. They were sitting at their table and the waiter was pouring champagne when Angela spotted the Delisis, who had just arrived in company with Philip Halliday. The professor stopped to greet someone he knew, while Mrs. Delisi glided across to say hallo, Halliday trailing in her wake. Sophia, looking stunning and not quite real, fell into conversation with Edgar, while Angela fought down the urge to pat her hair and peer at her reflection in a champagne-glass. At length the professor turned up, to Angela's surprise accompanied by Mr. Peterson, who was looking uncomfortable in an ill-fitting dinner-suit. Mrs.

Delisi turned her attention to her husband, who summoned a waiter and demanded more champagne.

'May I have the pleasure of the next one?' Halliday said to Angela. 'Or are you one of these women who will only dance with her husband?'

'Not at all,' she assured him, slightly relieved that Mrs. Delisi's presence had not rendered all men blind to her. 'I should be delighted.' She waited until Philip had turned away, then said to Edgar in an undertone, 'Go and dance with the divine Mrs. Delisi. Flirt with her and find out exactly how many of her lovers have died and the circumstances of their deaths.'

'I don't know that I want to take that sort of risk. What if she turns me to stone with her Medusa-like gaze?'

'I think you'll be safe enough, but I'll come and rescue you if I see her hair turning into live snakes.'

She went to join Philip on the floor, throwing a significant glance towards Mrs. Delisi as she did so.

'How are you today?' Philip asked as the dance began. 'Not too bruised from your fall yesterday?'

She could not have asked for a better opening.

'Quite well, thank you,' she replied. 'More embarrassed than anything else. I suppose both you and the professor arrived just in time to see me falling headlong in all my glory. Stupid of me: having seen the loose stones I ought to have had the sense not to stand directly under them. Did you see them fall?'

It was not exactly a subtle line of questioning, but she could not think of any other way to ask him.

'No, I didn't see anything but you—in fact I had no idea what had happened until I heard you shriek.'

'Did I shriek? I must have given you and the professor quite a fright. I suppose he was showing you around the fortress.'

'No, he wasn't. I was wandering around the hillside alone, turning over a few ideas in my head for my book. I didn't see Delisi until he turned up a minute after your fall.'

'Did you see anyone else nearby? I'd like to know how the stones came to fall off the wall.'

'Not that I recall,' he answered. 'You had a lucky escape, by the way.'

'So did Mr. Florakis. I think the shock of having two of his guests die in the same week might have finished him off,' she replied humorously. 'I hear the police believe Roy Cavell's death was an accident.'

His face darkened.

'Yes,' he said shortly.

She threw him a searching glance.

'Don't you agree?'

He was silent for a moment.

'I don't know,' he replied at last. 'I assumed it was at first, but then Peterson—who seems to fancy himself as a detective—started buzzing around talking about suicide, and I began to wonder.'

'Yes, he mentioned it to me too. He said it was because of Mrs. Delisi, although surely that's nonsense.'

He looked at her directly.

'Do you think so?'

'I don't know. I never met him, you see, so I have no way of judging whether he was the type to kill himself. What do you think?'

'I shouldn't be at all surprised to hear that Mrs. Delisi had driven a man to kill himself,' he replied acerbically. 'But whether Cavell was that man I couldn't tell you.'

Angela said lightly:

'These Greeks are very superstitious. Kostis told me he carries basil in his pocket to ward off evil spirits because he thinks Mrs. Delisi brings bad luck. It's all rot, of course.'

'Is it?'

'You don't appear convinced.'

He did not answer. She pressed him.

'On the day we found Cavell's body you said, "I knew she was bad luck." Were you referring to Mrs. Delisi?'

'Did I say that?' He grimaced, then seemed to shake himself. 'It's ridiculous—or at least it ought to be. I've always considered myself a rational sort of chap, but there's something about her—I don't know what it is.'

Angela could have told him what it was but did not.

'Perhaps I've been on this island too long and begun thinking as the locals do,' he said.

'You've gone native, do you mean?'

'If you like. Perhaps I've absorbed the superstition. But what is one to think when confronted with the facts?'

'And what are the facts?'

'That at least four men, including Roy Cavell, have died after associating with her. I don't know about evil spirits, but there seems to be a malign influence hanging about her.'

'Perhaps the professor has been doing away with all his rivals,' Angela suggested lightly.

She expected him to laugh but instead he frowned.

'What is it?' she asked.

'I don't know. I've just remembered something Roy said a few days before he died.' He thought. 'What was it? Yes —I remember now. He said there was something going on and that he meant to get to the bottom of it.'

'What was going on?'

'I don't know, but what you just said about Delisi made me think.'

'You don't mean to say Cavell really did suspect the

professor was responsible for the deaths of the men who died?'

She said it as a joke, for she did not want him to know she was serious about the idea.

'When you put it like that it sounds absurd.' He considered again, then shook his head. 'No, I don't think that's what he meant. At least, that's not the impression I got.'

'What do you think he did mean, then?'

'I rather thought it was something connected to the dig.'

'But what, exactly?'

'I'm not sure. To be perfectly honest it was late at night and I wasn't as sober as I ought to have been so I wasn't taking much in. I do remember he mentioned something about a letter from the governor about the head of a statue of Helios that he was expecting, which hadn't turned up, but I can't be certain it was part of the same conversation. He might have been referring to something else entirely.'

Angela remembered having seen the letter on Cavell's desk, and that Professor Delisi was in the habit of sending antiquities to the governor, who liked to display them at his house.

'And did the head turn up?' she asked.

'Not as far as I know. Cavell said his first thought was that it must have been sent to the museum in Rhodes by accident, or even to Athens. He was eternally exasperated at the disorganization up at the dig, incidentally. Delisi and Schulz are completely scatter-brained and don't write anything down properly. I dare say the head is in a box in a cupboard somewhere and will turn up sooner or later.'

The music came to an end and Philip escorted Angela back to her table. Edgar was not there. Angela sat down and thought of the note that had been pushed under her door. Was it connected to Roy's suspicions that something was going on at the dig? If so, presumably he had spoken to somebody about it, and the note was a reply. She did not have long to muse, however, for just then she was accosted by Mr. Peterson, who formally requested the pleasure of a dance. She agreed with a degree of trepidation that soon proved justified when she encountered Peterson's energetic but imprecise dancing steps. Angela maintained as much distance as she could from him and tried not to wince whenever he trod on her foot.

'This is a very opulent place,' opined Mr. Peterson as they moved around the floor. 'If you ask me, the people at the Acropolis ought to take a leaf from its book—the bedrooms here especially have little personal touches that they don't have at our hotel.'

'We came here first when we got off the ferry on Tuesday morning, but they didn't have room for us,' said Angela. 'Fortunately Edgar fell into conversation with Dr. Schulz in the lobby. He recommended St. Michael as a pleasant spot and kindly offered us a lift there.'

Peterson was looking wistfully at the chandeliers, to the further detriment of his concentration on the music.

'We never had anything like this in Andersville. It's quite an out-of-the-way place, close to the border with Kentucky, and very stifling for anyone with a sense of adventure. I always wanted to travel and see the world, but never thought I'd get to do it. Everyone laughed when I said I'd go to Europe one day. People used to laugh at me a lot.' He said it so bitterly that Angela would have felt sorry for him had he not just trodden on her foot for the fourth time. Then he brightened. 'Well, now they're laughing on the other side of their faces. Look at me here, dancing with a pretty lady in a fancy hotel on a Greek island.'

Angela acknowledged the compliment distractedly, for she had just spotted Edgar, who was still dancing with Mrs.

Delisi and clearly enjoying himself far too much. As the song ended and he brought Sophia back to her seat Angela drew him aside.

'That's quite enough of *that*, thank you,' she said firmly.

'I thought you told me to flirt with her.'

'I said flirt, not *canoodle*.'

'Canoodle? What an extraordinary word. I've never canoodled in my life—wouldn't have the first idea how to canoodle, in fact. Is it something one ought to learn? Perhaps you'd like to show me how to do it.'

'You know perfectly well what I meant,' she said severely.

'Hmph. You're no fun. And besides, you weren't doing too shabbily yourself, dancing with your tame author.'

'*Dancing*, yes. Because this is a dance. I danced with Philip and then I had to dance with Mr. Peterson and now my toes are very cross with me.'

'As bad as that, was it?' he said, amused.

'Apparently they don't teach a two-step in Andersville, Indiana. But never mind that—did you get anything out of her? Or were you too busy with other considerations?'

'Not a thing. She wouldn't give me an opening, and pretty much squashed me as soon as I got anywhere near the subject.'

'Really? My word! If you can't get it out of her then nobody can. Have you met your match at last?'

'I did ask the professor about yesterday though,' he said. 'After all, it's perfectly reasonable that a concerned husband would want to know why dangerously loose stones nearly fell on his wife's head at a dig Delisi was in charge of. He was very apologetic but insists he was nowhere near that wall and didn't see a thing.'

'I didn't do much better,' said Angela ruefully. 'I

wanted to question Philip discreetly but the questions came out of my mouth all wrong and sounded much too obvious. Luckily he didn't seem to notice. At any rate, I didn't get the impression he knew anything about my detecting, although he knew about Peterson's snooping around, and if he didn't know then why would he want to kill me?' She sighed. 'It might have been either of them, or even someone else entirely.'

'Or perhaps it was nobody.'

'It had occurred to me. The footprints might be a coincidence—after all, it could be that someone turned up, glanced over the wall and went away without trying to kill me. We're not doing very well, are we—look here, what are you doing?'

'Canoodling. This is how you do it, yes?'

'Stop it! This is a public place.'

'If one can't canoodle with one's own wife, then with whom *can* one canoodle?'

'Ass,' said Angela, half-laughing, looking around to make sure nobody was watching.

'Let's go outside,' he said. 'It's fearfully hot in here, and I need a breath of fresh air.'

They went out into the garden and found somewhere to sit. Edgar lit her a cigarette and they smoked companionably, listening to the sound of rushing waves from the sea nearby. Angela gazed thoughtfully at her cigarette and watched the smoke curling upward.

'I can't blame you for being drawn in by Sophia Delisi,' she said at last. 'She really is an exquisite creature.'

'She's a work of art, all right, but I shouldn't say there was anything especially fascinating about her personality. In fact, under the glitter she seems quite an ordinary girl. She wants what all other young women want—dancing, nice clothes, to be admired. Nothing unusual in that.'

'Then why is she married to the professor?'

'I expect that was her only choice. She's from a little village near Salonika where all the men fish and are very poor. Marrying Delisi was an escape of sorts, I imagine.'

She turned to him.

'Tell me truthfully—do you think I'm making too much of all this? Was Roy Cavell's death suspicious, or was it just an accident?'

'I don't know,' he replied. 'You're right when you say there are plenty of unanswered questions, but you've done all you can and proved nothing so far. And after yesterday I rather think it might be better to leave well alone.'

'Perhaps you're right,' she said.

Chapter Fifteen

But Angela could not leave well alone, because the next morning Miss Brinkhurst turned up in a most unexpected fashion. It was not long after breakfast, and Angela and Edgar had gone out to take a stroll along Archangel Beach. The day was breezy with a little cloud, and they had not got far from the hotel when they saw Dr. Schulz standing with two or three fisherman, among them Yannis. They were looking down at something that was concealed behind an expanse of flat rocks, and talking in urgent tones.

'Hallo, what's all this?' said Edgar.

Dr. Schulz glanced up as they drew near and shook his head warningly.

'Ach, no, you will not wish for your lady wife to see this,' he said.

There was no resisting such an invitation. Ignoring his words, Angela approached then stopped and put a hand to her mouth.

'Oh *no!*' she exclaimed.

Amy Brinkhurst was lying on her side crumpled up in a heap, her back resting against the rocks. Although her left arm was half-covering her face, there was no mistaking the bulk of her, or her wispy fair hair. The end of a pink scarf, patched with damp sand, trailed out from under her right shoulder.

'Not a drowning this time,' said Edgar grimly, indicating the scarf. 'She's been strangled.' He looked at Yannis. 'When did this happen?'

'I do not know,' replied Yannis. 'Dr. Schulz found her.'

Schulz rubbed the back of his neck in distress as he regarded the dreadful thing lying crumpled against the rock.

'This is the lady from the hotel, yes? She is the nurse of the one in the wheelchair, if I am not mistaken. This is a very terrible thing. We must report it immediately.'

'I think she's been missing since last night,' said Angela, suddenly remembering. 'I saw Lady Trenoweth looking for her.'

She stared at the body, taking in all the details. As Edgar had said, Miss Brinkhurst had certainly not drowned—even without the scarf twisted around her neck her clothes were dry and not disarranged in any way, and it was evident from her appearance that she had not been in the water.

Dr. Schulz turned and snapped out some directions in Greek to the fishermen.

'We will take her back to the hotel,' he said.

'You ought to leave her here for the police to see,' said Angela.

'Ach, yes, you are right. Yannis, you and the men will wait here, and I will go and telephone from the hotel.'

He hurried off, and Angela and Edgar followed more

slowly, since there was no question of their continuing their walk just now.

When they entered the hotel they found everything in confusion as Mr. Florakis bustled about, snapping out orders to his underlings and looking altogether as though he wanted to tear his hair out. It appeared the news had already spread to all the guests in the dining-room—thanks, they soon found out, to the good efforts of Mr. Peterson, who had been in the lobby when Dr. Schulz returned to report the calamity, and who had immediately assumed the mantle of hotel gossip following Miss Brinkhurst's unfortunate demise. The whole place was abuzz with talk, and all eyes were on Lady Trenoweth, who had planted herself in a chair by the desk, and was sitting very straight, an angry gleam in her eye. At last Mr. Florakis approached the old woman in the manner of one preparing to poke a ferocious tiger with a stick.

'The police will be here very soon,' he said. 'In the meantime, there is a woman from the village who will come and take care of you for the present.'

'That is all very well,' snapped Lady Trenoweth, 'but I need someone to accompany me back to England—preferably an English nurse, since I do not suppose these local women know the first thing about my condition.'

'Yes, yes—I will telephone and find such a person for you. In Rhodes there are many English, and most likely there will be a nurse to help you. If not, we can arrange for somebody to come from the mainland, or even from London. In the meantime we will do what we can, and you can be sure all will be well.'

'All will *not* be well,' she retorted. 'This disarranges my plans in a most inconvenient fashion.' Just then she spotted Angela. 'You there—Mrs. Merivale. One cannot always trust these foreigners to pass on information with any accuracy, but I understand you were present at the scene. They tell me my nurse has got herself killed. Is it true?'

'I'm afraid so. I'm terribly sorry.'

Lady Trenoweth drew herself up.

'Who did it?'

'I don't know.'

'Some local ne'er-do-well, no doubt. They must catch him, and quickly. This sort of thing cannot be allowed to go on.' She paused. 'How was she killed, exactly?'

'It looks as though she was strangled,' replied Angela.

'Cheated at the last!' said Lady Trenoweth obliquely. She pressed her lips together firmly, an expression of great annoyance on her face.

Angela glanced at her uncertainly then moved away, looking around for Edgar. She felt someone at her shoulder and turned to see Esther Grayson, who looked bewildered.

'Did you just say Miss Brinkhurst was strangled? How horrible!'

'It is, rather.'

'But how could it have happened?' Esther lowered her voice. 'And what does it all mean? First Roy, now this! Two deaths in one week can't be a coincidence, can it? I was so sure Roy killed himself, but then why is Miss Brinkhurst dead? Oh, Philip! Have you heard the news?'

Philip Halliday had just arrived, and joined them.

'What are all those police doing down on the beach?' he demanded.

He was informed of the terrible events, and whistled.

'My word! What the devil is going on in this accursed place? And what's Lady Trenoweth going to do now?'

'Oh, the poor thing, she must be desperate,' said Esther. 'I'll go and see if she needs anything.'

'Rather you than I,' observed Philip.

'We'd better go,' murmured Edgar into Angela's ear.

'There's nothing we can do and we'll only be getting in the way. Let's go and have our walk by the harbour instead.'

Angela assented in silence and they went out.

'Well, that's put the cat among the pigeons,' he said, as they walked down the rocky path. 'Poor Miss Brinkhurst— she won't even have the fun of gossiping about her own death this evening at dinner.' He threw Angela a glance. 'Still, it looks as though you were right all along, and that Cavell really was murdered. I bow to your superior detective ability—assuming, that is, that we don't have two murderers on the loose. That really would be the limit.'

She was not in the mood for his cheerfulness, for a profusion of disturbing ideas had been tumbling higgledy-piggledy through her mind for the past hour. Her first thought on witnessing the scene down on the beach had been a purely selfish one—that she had left it too late, and would never now be able to make her confession to Miss Brinkhurst. Quite aside from the evil of the murder itself, whoever had killed the nurse had added insult to injury and cheated Angela out of her ability to make up for her own wrongdoing. For half a moment on the beach earlier a mad thought had darted into her head that Miss Brinkhurst had done it on purpose purely to spite her. It had passed immediately, but even now her mind was still in a tumult. Miss Brinkhurst had been an odious scandal-monger, but she ought not to have ended up dead behind a rock, being gawped at by a gaggle of curious fishermen. Angela felt an anger welling up inside her that she could not quite explain. She was furious at the murderer for having killed Miss Brinkhurst, and furious at Miss Brinkhurst for having provoked it—for there was no doubt in her mind that the woman had brought it on herself in some way. But most of all she was furious at herself for her cowardice of the other day, and for not having found out who had killed Roy Cavell in time to prevent this latest death.

Edgar, meanwhile, seemed not in the least disturbed by the events of the morning, and as Angela brooded silently he strolled by her side as though he had not a care in the world, to her intense annoyance. In fact, as is the way of things, her anger had begun to shift irrationally away from herself and towards her husband, since had it not been for him and his notorious history she would not be in this wretched position at all. But there he was, smiling and enjoying the sunshine as though this were quite an ordinary honeymoon and they were quite an ordinary couple. He stopped to watch an old Greek fisherman mending his net, admired a boat as it pulled into the harbour, then dug into his pocket for his cigarette-case. This last action was the final straw.

'If you really want me to be a good little wife and put on a pretence that you've pulled the wool over my eyes you might at least have the decency to keep those things out of my sight,' she said sharply.

He paused in the act of lighting the cigarette, surprised.

'What?'

'Those cigarettes. Don't think I don't know what you've been up to.'

His face took on a closed, expressionless look, and all of a sudden she was reminded of the old Edgar, in the days when he was bad.

'Go on, then. What *have* I been up to?' he said.

'Helping Yannis smuggle tobacco. I'm right, aren't I?'

She had not intended to confront him about it, but the words were out now and it was too late to take them back. He did not reply, and she went on:

'I saw the boxes in the cabin of his boat the other day.

The labels were in Turkish but I could see what it was. He brought an illegal cargo in and you pretended to the police we were going out for a pleasure-trip to stop them searching his boat. On the journey back I saw the boxes were gone, so presumably he found somewhere to unload them. You've been smoking those cigarettes since the day we went to Lindos. That's where you got them, isn't it—from Yannis. I've never seen them in the shops.'

He looked at the cigarette in his hand.

'Don't you like them? They're ten times better than the official ones.'

'That's not the point!' she exclaimed, exasperated. 'You're not supposed to be doing this sort of thing any more.'

'I'm not "doing this sort of thing", as you put it. I did him a favour to get him out of a fix, that's all.'

'But why did he need your help? Why did he bring the stuff into shore in broad daylight in the first place?'

He was looking at her assessingly.

'He was meant to bring it in the night before but couldn't, because the *carabinieri* were buzzing around in the hotel and down by the shore after Cavell's death,' he said at last. 'We had to warn him to stay away.'

'We?'

'Kostis and I.'

'Is that where you were when you disappeared the other night?'

'Yes. Those two Italians in the bar were running Kostis off his feet. He'd already been up to the acropolis once to signal to Yannis and warn him not to come in, but they were showing no signs of going home so I said I'd go up to signal again for him. Yannis got the message and went further down the coast to unload the stuff at the house of a cousin of his. But he couldn't get the fellow to wake up, and it was too dangerous to leave it outside somewhere, so he brought it into the harbour the next morning and hoped for the best. It was just unfortunate that the police turned up while we were there and I had to do some quick thinking.'

'So you pretended the trip was for my benefit.'

'It was for your benefit. You had fun, didn't you? And so did I. And we got Yannis out of a tight spot, so everybody's happy.'

'Except me. It's the *deceit* I hate,' she said. 'You said you wouldn't lie to me.'

'I haven't lied—well, not very much,' he corrected himself as she opened her mouth to speak. 'The story about losing my pocket-book was a fib, I'll grant you that —but only a little one.'

His shameless admission did nothing to soothe her. Before she could stop herself, she burst out indignantly:

'And all this time I've been feeling terrible because Miss Brinkhurst told me she knew who I was and I denied it. But there was no need for me to feel guilty at all, was there? Because you haven't changed one bit.'

She wished she had not said it, but the words were out of her mouth now.

'You denied it? Oh, so that's what all this is about,' he said, suddenly understanding. He gave a disbelieving laugh. 'You're not angry with me at all—you're angry with yourself.'

She ignored him and went on:

'And another thing—how do you know Kostis and Yannis? You've been talking to them like old friends ever since we got here. In fact, was this ever meant to be a honeymoon at all? It was your suggestion we come to Rhodes. Was it really for me, or did you have something else in mind?'

'Of course it was for you.'

'*Only* for me?' she insisted.

For a few moments he said nothing, seeming to debate something within himself. Then he sighed.

'Come with me. I want to introduce you to someone,' he said.

Chapter Sixteen

THE SOMEONE LIVED in a tiny house at the end of a narrow cobbled alleyway in St. Michael—so narrow that the sun's rays did not reach as far as the ground. Edgar knocked at a door whose paint was chipped and peeling, then opened it and called out something in Greek.

'Mind your head,' he said.

They ducked through the low doorway then went down three steps and into a room that was pitch-dark after the glare of the sun outside. As Angela's eyes slowly adjusted to the dim light she distinguished a room with a floor that was part earth, part tiles. A table and chairs stood in the corner to her left, with a rickety old dresser behind it stacked with plates, cups and many other odds and ends. A smell of stale lamb fat emanated from a pot on a stove at the far end of the room. To her right a flight of stairs led up into darkness. Ahead of her a tiny window looked out on to the street, streaked with the dirt and smoke of years. Although dust had collected in the corners and one or two cobwebs hung from the ceiling, it looked as though some hurried attempts had been made to keep the main parts of the room clean. Under the window an old man lay in bed, propped up against a heap of pillows.

'The house isn't in the best shape,' said Edgar. 'His wife died years ago and there are no daughters to look after the place for him—only Kostis and Yannis, who are out most of the time. Hallo, Georgios, you old devil. How are you today. Any better? I've brought my wife to meet you.'

'Your wife?' The old man struggled to sit up. 'Give me a hand with these pillows, won't you?' he said to Angela.

She helped plump up the pillows so he could sit up. The bed-linen was crisp and white and bore a suspicious resemblance to the sheets at the Hotel Acropolis. The effort of moving had caused the old man to cough and wheeze. He seemed in a bad way, although his glittering black eyes indicated that there was life in him yet. His accent was Greek with a touch of Brooklyn.

'You shoulda let me know you were coming. I get the butler and the maid-servants in to clean the place, yes? Bring out the best silver.' His eyes examined Angela from head to foot. 'A wife, eh? You never told me you brought a wife with you.' He gave a wheezy laugh. 'You're a fine woman. What are you doing taking a bad one like this one, eh?'

'You may well ask,' said Edgar. 'Angela, this is Georgios. In case you hadn't guessed it, he's the father of Kostis and Yannis, and formerly—since you're bound to ask sooner or later—the most expert forger of jewels in Zurich. Nobody could make a more convincing diamond necklace than he could.'

'Those were fine days,' said the old man. 'No more, though. Everything comes to an end sooner or later. It was good of you to come and see old Georgios again. Get the bottle, yes? Over there on the table. We will have the retsina and toast one last time before I die.'

'One last time, then another, and another. Your sort don't die,' said Edgar. 'You're as tough as old boots. I'm more likely to go before you do.'

He fetched a bottle and poured out three glasses of yellow liquid into tumblers which Angela also recognized as having come from the hotel. She sipped at it gingerly while Edgar and Georgios talked over old times.

'Remember that job we did in Geneva, eh?' said Georgios. 'That old countess—what was her name again? The one who looked like a horse. They never did find out what happened. But maybe better not talk about it in front of the lady.'

'Better not. I've retired now and she doesn't exactly approve of it.'

Georgios leered at Angela.

'You're keeping him straight, eh? A good thing too. It doesn't pay in the end. I had plenty of money when I was in the game—cars, women, a house, anything I wanted—but look at me now. You were better off getting out while you could,' he said to Edgar.

There came the sound of voices outside, then the door opened and Yannis entered, accompanied by another young man. Yannis stopped when he saw Angela and looked at Edgar inquiringly.

'I'm afraid Angela's rumbled us,' said Edgar. 'She saw the goods on the boat the other day.'

'No flies on her, eh?' wheezed Georgios.

Yannis gave a sheepish grin.

'It was only a little job. Lucky for me you were there.' He indicated his companion. 'But not so lucky for me that Nikos wasn't at home the night before.'

'He wasn't at *his* home,' said Georgios slyly. 'He went into the wrong house by accident and fell asleep in the bed of Polina while her husband was away.'

Nikos made some protestation as Yannis cuffed him over the ear, and there was much chaffing in Greek of a ribald nature, to judge by their gestures. They talked a while longer, then Georgios began to get tired so Angela and Edgar took their leave.

'So that's who you came to see,' said Angela as they left the house. 'I wondered where you'd kept disappearing to. I suppose the honeymoon was merely an afterthought, was it?'

'Of course not. If you remember, we never intended to come on honeymoon at all. The trip to Greece was quite above the board—you don't really think I arranged for that reporter fellow to turn up and start pestering us, do you? But then we got to Athens and didn't like it much, so I got the idea of coming to Rhodes instead. I'd met an old acquaintance in Clairvaux who knew Georgios and told me he was in a bad way, you see, so I thought it couldn't hurt to come and look him up one last time to say goodbye. You can see for yourself he hasn't got long left. I didn't mention him before because I didn't think you'd want to meet him, but I'd never have dreamt of suggesting we come here if I hadn't thought you'd like it too.'

'Oh.' She was only moderately reassured, but decided not to press the matter. 'Is Georgios a good friend of yours?'

'Let's say he got me out of a jam a few times. I can't vouch for his honesty or his uprightness as you'd call it, but he was good to me at a bad time—and I'm rather afraid helped set me off on the wrong path.'

'And Kostis and Yannis are bringing goods into the country illegally and following in his footsteps.'

'There's not a Greek on Rhodes who isn't doing something to try and put one over on the Italians,' he replied. 'The smuggling is just a way to make a bit of extra money.'

'That doesn't make it right,' she pointed out.

'You're not above drinking cocktails in New York. Where do you think the gin comes from?'

'That's different,' said Angela, somewhat feebly. 'Everybody does it.'

'Exactly my point, so don't be a prig. At any rate, if you've been fretting that I'm falling back into the old ways, I assure you there's no need. I did them a favour the other day because if Yannis and Kostis end up in gaol there'll be no-one to look after Georgios, that's all.'

'Don't tell me you didn't enjoy it, though.'

'Of course I did. I never denied that I like a little danger. I'll never be the sort to sit at home in front of a fire, smoking a pipe, but you knew that perfectly well when you married me—in fact I rather thought that was what you liked about me. You don't want a quiet life either. Try and deny it all you like but you crave excitement just as much as I do. That's why we're so well suited—I thought you understood that.'

She was silenced, because he was right, of course. It was very provoking.

'But you can't have it both ways,' he went on. 'You can't be ostentatiously respectable *and* have all the fun too. Look here, you have a choice: take me as I am or spend the rest of your life regretting this. I'm doing the best I can, and that's the most I can promise.'

He was not the sort to abase himself before her, so it was the nearest she was likely to get to an apology.

'And anyway, what about your side of the bargain?' he continued pointedly. 'You said you'd never be ashamed of me but you fell at the first fence.'

She also had her pride, but an explanation was due.

'I didn't mean to do it, truly I didn't. She caught me when I wasn't expecting it, that's all. She was quite beastly.

She slunk towards me and made all sorts of horrid insinuations, and I got such a surprise I told her she was talking nonsense before I knew what I was doing. I've been trying to get hold of her for days to tell her the truth, but there was never a moment, and now it's too late.'

They had reached the harbour now and stood in silence for a few minutes, watching the seagulls wheel and swoop over the water. At last Edgar sighed.

'Damn. We seem to have got off on the wrong foot, don't we? I did mean to be good.' He turned to her and took both her hands. 'Shall we start again?'

'Yes please,' she said.

'Good. We'll get it right this time.'

Chapter Seventeen

'So then, to return to the murder of Miss Brinkhurst,' said Edgar, as they resumed their walk. 'Do you have any thoughts on the matter?'

'Only that she must have known something about Roy Cavell's death,' replied Angela.

'And presumably taunted the murderer about it. That's hardly a surprise—the woman had blackmailer written all over her. Do you think she was hoping to blackmail you?'

'I assume so. She was called away before we could continue our conversation, but I was half-expecting her to come to me later and make some demand or other.' She made an impatient noise. 'Drat the woman! Why did she have to go and get herself killed? I was *so* looking forward to telling her to publish and be damned.'

'That's my girl! And if Miss Brinkhurst was the sort to blackmail, then she was almost certainly dangling other victims from a string too. But who?'

'The professor and Dr. Schulz,' said Angela, stopping suddenly. 'One or the other of them, at any rate.'

'What?'

'I've just remembered something Philip told me last night. He said Roy suspected something untoward was going on up at the excavations. I'd been meaning to think about it this morning but Miss Brinkhurst put everything else out of my mind.'

'What do you mean, "untoward"?'

'He didn't know exactly. Apparently Cavell had mentioned something about the head of a statue that was supposed to be sent to the governor's house but went missing, but Philip couldn't say for certain whether that was connected to Roy's suspicions. It sounds as if it might have been, though.'

'Dear me, has somebody been snaffling the antiquities, do you suppose?'

'I wonder. Remember the note under the door? It was typed in the office, and I rather think that's what it referred to. What if Cavell had spoken of his suspicions to someone up at the dig and this was the reply?'

'That makes much more sense than your theory about Delisi wreaking merciless vengeance upon all the rivals for his wife's affections.'

'Perhaps the idea was a little far-fetched,' she admitted. 'But which of them wrote the note? It must be one of the two men. Cavell suspected one of them was up to something and spoke to the other one about it.'

'Must it be Delisi or Schulz? It might have been Miss Grayson who wrote it.'

'I don't think so. The language is too formal and stilted for that. Besides, can you see Esther typing him a note? She'd have written it by hand if anything, or more likely spoken to him in person.'

'True. Let's take it as a working hypothesis, then, since we've nothing better to go on. Cavell suspected either the professor or Dr. Schulz of stealing relics, and mentioned it to the other one, who wrote him a note to say that everything was explained and to warn him to keep quiet. Which of them is it, though?'

Angela thought.

'At a guess I'd say the professor was the thief and that Cavell talked to Schulz about it,' she said at last. 'Remember the note said that speaking out would only cause trouble—and who would cause the bigger scandal if it turned out they'd been stealing things? Why, Professor Delisi, of course—he's a world-renowned archaeologist, here by appointment of the Italian government. Something like this could ruin the reputation of all sorts of academic institutions and would be a terrible embarrassment to Italy. Dr. Schulz is a nobody by comparison. If he was suspected of some crime then the professor wouldn't worry about the trouble it would cause—he'd just swat Schulz away like a troublesome fly.'

'You don't like the professor much, do you?'

'I don't like or dislike him, but I certainly shouldn't like to cross him. And I imagine everyone up at the dig felt the same way. If Cavell had suspicions he'd naturally want to tread carefully before throwing accusations around publicly.'

'But he must have accused the professor directly at some point, or why was he killed? Or did Schulz snitch to him about Cavell's suspicions?'

'I doubt it, else surely he would have had to kill Schulz too.' She pondered. 'Is it enough of a motive, do you think? Are antiquities worth the bother? Is there much money in them?'

'To the right customer they're worth the bother,' he assured her. 'There are any number of enthusiasts who are willing to pay a pretty penny for the things they like, and who aren't interested in looking too closely into their provenance.'

'I'll take your word for it since you're the expert.'

Edgar felt in his pocket for a cigarette but thought better of it.

'So where does Miss Brinkhurst come in?' he said. 'Following on from our theory, let's say for argument's sake that she was blackmailing Professor Delisi and he killed her. Was it because she'd found out about his illegal activities, or because she knew he'd killed Roy Cavell?'

'Either or both. I wonder how she knew, though.' She had a sudden thought. 'Of course! She found the evidence in Roy's trunk!'

'You mean you think she was the one who searched through his luggage?'

'Yes! I'm almost sure of it,' she said eagerly. 'In fact, I think I gave her the idea myself. I mentioned that the police had probably searched the trunk, and she gave me an awfully funny look as though she'd just had an idea. I'll bet she crept into the store-room and had a good rummage through his things.'

'It's possible,' he conceded.

'Well somebody certainly did it, and we've agreed she's the type.'

'Yes, I can see her doing it. Very well, assuming you're right, the question is: what did she find?'

'I don't know. A list of missing antiquities? Or perhaps even some evidence that Professor Delisi had something to do with the death of his wife's first husband,' she added hopefully.

'Still harping on that theory, are you?'

'I was rather fond of it, but I won't insist on it.'

'If Miss Brinkhurst searched the trunk, did she also

steal the brown leather valise Cavell was going to take to Athens?' said Edgar.

'That's a thought. We might try and find out when we get back to the hotel. How can we get into her room? It would be too marvellous if we could find the blackmail material she'd been using.'

'I shouldn't bank on it. Surely the first thing the murderer would do after killing her would be to find it and take or destroy it.'

'Well, we'll see. Now, is there anything else we haven't thought of?'

'Where does the scrap of hotel note-paper we found on the cliff top come in?' said Edgar. 'And the letter from Cavell's friend that you seemed to think was important?'

'I'd forgotten about those. I expect the scrap of paper has nothing to do with anything—unless it was torn from the letter itself and fell out of his pocket while he was walking, or something like that. Sophia did say Roy's friend was over in London, and I suppose he might have written from the Savoy since he was meant to be rich. But I should say it's more likely the letter is in the brown suitcase—wherever that is.'

Edgar frowned.

'This theory of ours depends on a lot of assumptions. In fact, I'd call it a little unwieldy. Why hasn't Schulz spoken up before now? If he knew Cavell suspected the professor of stealing you'd think he'd have mentioned it after Cavell turned up dead. I mean to say, surely he wouldn't have kept a murder quiet?'

'Remember not everyone has our nasty suspicious minds, and most people still believe Roy's death was an accident. As a matter of fact, I expect Schulz was rather relieved to get Cavell and his suspicions off his back, since reporting the professor would have caused no end of a stink—and perhaps even done him out of a job.'

'But the note said "all is explained." That implies Schulz had looked into the matter and decided there'd been a dreadful misunderstanding, and that Delisi had shoved all the gold pendants and painted amphorae absent-mindedly into a box under his desk and forgotten about them. Does that mean nobody was stealing anything at all? How easy would it be to spirit things away, incidentally?'

'As easy as anything, given their disorganization,' replied Angela. 'Esther was trying to type up some pages the other day, and could make neither head nor tail of the lists. There's nothing to stop anybody taking whatever they wanted away with them, but if they were keeping proper records it would be noticed. Roy was paying attention, though, and presumably noticed something amiss.'

'I wonder how the professor got the stuff off the island, then. Did he pack it up and send it by post, do you suppose?'

'You'd better ask Yannis that,' said Angela suddenly.

'What?'

'If I'm not much mistaken it's not only tobacco he's been smuggling. I've just remembered something else I saw on the boat the other day. There was a crate full of packing materials and straw. It's the same stuff they use up at the dig—you know, that yellowish paper with the printing down one side. I'm sure it can't be a coincidence. I'll bet you any money that's how the things were spirited out.'

'I hope you don't think it's anything to do with me,' he said. 'All I wanted was a decent cigarette. I'm not interested in broken vases.'

'Perhaps it's just a coincidence. Do you think Yannis would confess to it if we asked him?'

'Not if he thinks you're going to report it.'

This was a tricky one. She wanted to find out whether her suspicions were true, but having been admitted into the confidence of Georgios and his family, she could hardly then use the knowledge against them. Angela put the matter to the back of her mind for the moment.

'Well, let's see if we can find that brown leather suitcase at last,' she said. 'Perhaps that will give us some answers.'

Chapter Eighteen

THEY RETURNED to the hotel and found it occupied by the Italian police, who were striding about officiously in their smart uniforms. Mr. Florakis wore his usual ingratiating smile, but it was quivering slightly at the edges, and altogether he had the air of one whose patience has been sorely tried.

'Which floor was she on?' said Edgar as they entered the lobby.

'This one—I expect because of the wheelchair,' replied Angela.

She led the way along a corridor towards the room to which she had taken Lady Trenoweth a few days ago. Presumably Miss Brinkhurst had been situated in a room close by. They found it immediately, for the door was open and uniformed men were going in and out of it.

'Bother!' muttered Angela. 'I suppose we oughtn't to have expected to breeze in just like that. Now what do we do?'

Edgar approached the nearest policeman and spoke to him in Italian, then returned, shaking his head.

'No go,' he said briefly as they returned to the lobby.

'What did you say to him?'

'I told him we'd lent her a brown leather suitcase and we'd like it back once they've finished with it. He said there wasn't any such thing in her room, then sent me off with a flea in my ear and as good as told me to keep my nose out.'

'Oh dear. It doesn't look as though we'll get much from this end of things if the police are in charge, does it? Well, if she doesn't have the brown suitcase and they won't let us look through her luggage we'll have to find some other way of finding out what she knew. That means going back up to the dig.'

'Is that a good idea? Remember we're dealing with someone who has already killed at least once, quite possibly twice, and has also had a go at you. Our murderer is obviously the kind of person who has absolutely no compunction about putting someone out of the way if it serves his or her ends. Besides, as you can see, the police are looking into it now.'

They were approached just then by Mr. Peterson, who was in a great state of agitation.

'Have you heard the news?' he said breathlessly. 'They've arrested two local fishermen on suspicion of murdering poor Miss Brinkhurst!'

'Already?' said Angela in surprise. 'Why should they have killed her?'

'That's what I've been wondering. Kostis seems to think they've been in trouble with the police before, for theft.'

'But theft isn't murder, is it?'

'No, but perhaps they stole something from her. Robbery's a good enough motive for killing.' He glanced towards the corridor from which Angela and Edgar had just emerged. 'They're searching her room right now, but I guess you saw them. Did you ask to help too?'

'Not exactly,' replied Angela, slightly irked at the suggestion she had been chasing after the police and begging to join in their games.

Peterson went on:

'I offered my assistance but they sent me away. Imagine that!' He looked at her curiously. 'I don't suppose they told you anything useful?'

'No.'

'You will let me know if you find anything out, won't you? We could join forces if you like.' He clasped his hands together beatifically. 'Can you imagine how overjoyed they'd be if we presented them with the murderer?'

Angela could imagine they would not be overjoyed at all to have two amateur detectives meddling in their investigation, but did not say so. Peterson wandered off, and Angela looked at Edgar.

'I suppose I really ought to go and tell them what we know,' she said. 'They can't just go around arresting fishermen as the mood takes them.'

'What if the fishermen did it?'

'Perhaps they did, but the police ought to consider all the evidence first.'

'There isn't much evidence to consider, but you may as well try.'

Angela did so. The chief of police was very polite, but it was clear that he had no time for abstruse theories from idle dilettantes. Did the *signora* have any proof that the unfortunate death of Mr. Cavell earlier in the week was also murder, or that it had any connection to the dreadful killing of Miss Brinkhurst? Alas, the suspected absence of a suitcase and a note under the door were not enough to indicate such a thing, and the *signora* must understand that the police could not go about making accusations of this nature without some proper evidence. As to her little adventure at the archaeological excavation on Friday, he was sorry that she had narrowly avoided being injured by the falling wall, but delighted to hear she had come to no harm. The fortress was an ancient building, and it was understandable that some of the stones should have come loose. He would certainly look into the matter if the *signora* had any proof that somebody had pushed them off the wall deliberately, but in the meantime, if she would excuse him for contradicting a lady, he was of the opinion that it had most likely been an accident.

Angela gave it up and returned to her husband.

'No use?' he asked.

'No, and I can't blame him. It sounded feeble even to me when I was telling him. I couldn't mention my suspicions about what's been going on at the dig since it's pure guess-work on my part, and the rest sounded like so much speculation based on very little evidence. He as good as told me to go away and paint my nails.'

'Shouldn't you rather do that?'

'No thank you.'

'Well, there's not much more we can do today, with these fellows buzzing around, so why don't we go and take a dip?'

It was the first time they had been in the pool since the day of her shocking encounter with Roy Cavell. She had thought she might have been put off by the experience, but when they arrived they saw a number of other guests already enjoying themselves noisily in the water, and she found it was not difficult at all to forget what had happened. She sat in the shallows as she had the other day, and reflected upon the events of the morning, and what Edgar had said to her down by the harbour. They had made it up for now, but it was becoming clear that their marriage was always going to be a series of delicate negotiations. Was this the case for other couples? Her previous marriage had been a resounding failure from the start so she had no idea. Of course, most people were not married to recently retired criminals, and so probably did not have this additional factor to consider.

Angela had never given much philosophical thought to the nature of good and evil before, for the difference between the two had always seemed clear to her, and in those tricky instances where she had herself done something that was not quite above the board, she had always been very good at putting it to the back of her mind, or at finding an excuse as to why the rules did not apply to her in that particular case. But now she was married to Edgar she was beginning to realize that she would have to come to terms with the many shades of grey that lay between the black and the white, and the fact that his view of what was good and what was bad might often differ from hers. It would be a new lesson for her, but having chosen to marry him she had no choice but to learn it if she wanted the marriage to be a success.

He had been swimming, but now came to join her in the shallows.

'All right? Not brooding, I trust? I mean, this whole thing hasn't ruined the honeymoon for you, has it?'

'No,' she said.

'Look here,' he went on. 'I know I was a little unfeeling about Miss Brinkhurst this morning, but I hope you don't think I approve of strangling tiresome women.'

'I know perfectly well you don't.'

'Good. Don't forget it.' He looked at her curiously. 'What are you smiling at?'

'Nothing,' she said.

By Monday the problem of Lady Trenoweth's nurse had still not been resolved. The woman from St. Michael could not come, it turned out, and none of the maids who worked at the hotel had been able to suit the imperious guest. They were still trying to find an English attendant in Rhodes or elsewhere, but in the meantime Lady Trenoweth had, somewhat surprisingly, taken a liking to Esther Grayson, who had kept her company the previous day.

'She's not an awful person,' Esther confided to Angela, 'but she's in pain a lot of the time, which makes her bad-tempered. I don't mind that, and I seem to be able to manage her, but I don't know what she's going to do today without me. I'm wanted up at the dig, you see—the professor needs me to finish typing up his catalogue for the exhibition, because he wants to get it sent off to Athens by the end of tomorrow, and there's such a lot still to do. I wish we could find somebody to take care of poor Lady Trenoweth today, until we can find her a proper nurse.'

She eyed Angela speculatively. Angela did not take the hint, for the last thing she wanted was to spend the day catering to the whims of a peevish old woman. However, an idea came to her.

'I wonder,' she ventured. 'What if I did the typing for you? Then you could stay with Lady Trenoweth. Would the professor mind, do you think?'

'You?' said Esther, looking at her doubtfully. It was obvious she did not think Angela was the working sort. 'Do you know how to use a typewriter?'

'Pitman-trained, believe it or not,' replied Angela. 'My record was one hundred and eleven words per minute. That was a long time ago, of course, but I dare say I could still manage seventy or eighty with a following wind. What do you think?'

'But you're not here to work.'

'No, I'm not—but if it's just a question of lending a hand for a day until they can get somebody in to see to Lady Trenoweth, I don't mind at all. Besides, I had such a marvellous time up at the dig the other day I'd love to visit it again and take a closer look at all the beautiful old vases and things.'

She grimaced inwardly at the inanity of her last comment, but Esther did not seem to suspect anything.

'I'd have to ask the professor,' she said.

'Splendid. Then it's settled. I'll get your catalogue ready for you, and you can keep Lady Trenoweth company. I'm sure she'll be delighted to have you.'

The professor, it appeared, had no interest in who did his typing, so long as it was done. Accordingly, Angela once again found herself up at the dig, sitting at Miss Grayson's desk in the office that had once been occupied by Roy Cavell. Edgar had been reluctant to allow her to go, and made a half-hearted attempt to assert his authority and forbid it until she pointed out that since he had insisted she take him for what he was, it was only fair that the reverse also apply. He was forced to admit the justice of her assertion.

'What are you, though?' he said, regarding her consideringly. 'A dog that won't let go of a bone, I suppose.'

'I should prefer to call myself a seeker after truth rather than a dog, but if you like.'

'Well, then, if you're really determined to go I'll come with you.'

'As a sort of bodyguard, do you mean? Won't you be bored, waiting about all day?'

'I'll be even more bored having to suffer my own company all alone for the next few years if somebody finally succeeds in bouncing a rock off your head.'

'A fair point. I don't think it will happen, but I won't decline the offer. Thank you, darling.'

So Edgar sat outside in the sun, watching the men busy themselves sifting through the earth in the foundations of the ancient temple, and occasionally casting an eye back through the door of the hut at his wife as she rattled away on the old typewriter. Angela had hoped to give him Esther's lists and set him to work looking through the collections to see if anything was missing, but unfortunately for her purposes she could not get rid of Professor Delisi and Dr. Schulz, who seemed to have settled themselves in the office for the morning. Neither she nor Edgar would be able to go and do any detecting while they were there, so she had no choice but to keep working and hope they would leave her alone sooner or later.

At last her wishes were rewarded when Professor Delisi rose and said that he intended to go into Rhodes for some supplies. There was some little fuss as he and Dr. Schulz talked over what was to be got, then he went out and Angela heard the sound of a car starting and an engine fading into the distance. Now only Schulz remained. To her joy he shortly afterwards went to the door and asked Edgar if he would like to see the inscriptions they had found at the North side of the temple. Edgar professed himself only too willing to be educated, and the two men went off. Angela gave it a minute then rose and went into the long room in which most of the collections were kept. Between them, Roy and Esther had managed to keep the objects in some kind of order, so Angela took the lists and counted off as many things as she could, thankful that Esther had also typed a separate list of the things that had been sent to the governor's house, which would naturally be absent from the collection here. She soon established that there was nothing missing from the main room—at least, not according to the typed lists. Only the hand-written lists that Esther had showed her the other day remained. Where were those objects? Angela looked around. At the far end of the room next to the door to the dark-room was another door. She opened it and found it led into a large store-cupboard lined with shelves stacked high with boxes. More boxes stood on the floor. Angela glanced into one and saw a jumble of bits of pot, worn tools and beads, thrown in carelessly with seemingly no sense of order or neatness. Angela's heart sank. How was she ever meant to find anything here?

She squinted at the scrawled pages. As far as she could make out there were several things that were too big to be put in boxes. They were not in the main room, so by rights they ought to be here in the cupboard. In addition, some-body had at least taken care to store the gold jewellery separately in a wooden box, so it ought to be possible to find what she was looking for. A quick hunt soon told her that an 18-inch section of decorative stone-work and a well-preserved amphora painted with a hunting scene were not there. In addition, as far as she could tell from the most clearly written note-pages, at least one gold pendant was missing.

Angela chewed her lip. Edgar had joked about the professor having absent-mindedly hidden gold pendants and painted amphorae under his desk, but he could not possibly have known that those particular things were missing because he had been smuggling cigarettes, not stealing antiquities. She was sure that gold pendants and painted amphorae were two a penny at archaeological digs, so it was almost certainly a coincidence. Pushing the thought firmly to the back of her mind, she turned back to her task. The pages with many crossings-out were more difficult to decipher, but if somebody had been stealing then that was probably deliberate. What better way to spirit things out from under everybody's nose than by writing everything down so badly that nobody could possibly keep track of everything?

She was so absorbed in her task that she did not hear the motor approaching or the sound of footsteps coming towards the hut until it was too late. Only the sound of the outside door of the hut opening made her jump and alerted her to the danger. At first she thought it was Edgar, returning with Dr. Schulz, and for the first few seconds she did not worry too much, since she knew that on finding her missing from the office Edgar was perfectly capable of thinking of some hasty excuse to get Schulz out of the way and allow her to leave the cupboard without being discovered. But there were no voices, and she knew then that it was not Edgar and Dr. Schulz.

Angela's heart began to thump in her breast, although she was not sure why. There was no good reason for her to be in this cupboard, but equally there was no reason why she should not come in and look at the collection. But she was alone with an unknown person, only a few days after someone had tried to kill her here at the dig. Edgar, who was supposed to be protecting her, had gone off with Dr. Schulz.

She heard the squeak of the office door and the footsteps stopped for a second. Angela imagined the visitor looking in and finding the room empty. Then the footsteps started again, more slowly this time. They were coming towards her. Angela decided to brazen it out.

She put down the notebook on a shelf so as not to arouse suspicion of her activities, and stepped smartly out of the cupboard. Professor Delisi stopped in surprise.

'Oh, I thought you'd gone!' she exclaimed brightly.

'Yes, I realized I had forgotten to tell Schulz something, but he is not here.' He was looking at her curiously.

'I've nearly finished typing up the catalogue and I was wondering whether there was anything else I could do,' she explained, gesturing towards the cupboard. 'Miss Grayson told me things were a little untidy here and I thought I might put them into some kind of order. But I think it might be beyond the work of one day,' she added with a pleasant smile.

'Ah, yes,' said the professor. 'I am afraid you will find us sadly disarranged.'

His manner was perfectly polite and there was no sense of threat, but still Angela would have preferred not to be in the room alone with him. He was standing between her and the door, and she was just wondering how to make an excuse to get past him when to her enormous relief Edgar arrived, followed by Dr. Schulz.

'There you are,' said the professor to Schulz. 'I forgot to mention…'

The two men went outside and Edgar muttered:

'Sorry, I was at the other side of the temple when the car arrived, and that fellow *would* keep me talking. He didn't try anything funny, I suppose?'

'Not at all—in fact he looked nothing more than slightly surprised. Listen, I've only two more pages to do then we can go.'

She fetched Miss Grayson's notebook from inside the cupboard and replaced it in the drawer from which she had taken it, then finished her work quickly.

'So, what did you find?' asked Edgar when they arrived back at the hotel.

'Some things are almost certainly missing,' she replied.

'Stolen, do you think?'

'I can't say for sure, but I believe so. There's a pattern

to it, you see. For example, according to the lists there ought to have been three bits of stone-work, but there are only two; five pendants but there are only four; three amphorae but there are only two, and so on. They weren't described in much detail in the records, and sometimes the numbers were crossed out or unclear, so it would be easy to overlook them. If there wasn't more than one of a thing it was left alone.'

'Take one of several and it's less likely to be noticed,' he said, nodding. 'The oldest trick in the book. So now what?'

'We really ought to speak to Yannis. As you said, the missing antiquities might just have been accidentally mislaid, so we need proof they were taken deliberately.'

'And if we don't get it?'

'Then there's nothing else to be done and we leave the police to do their job. But if we do…'

She stopped.

'What?'

'Well, we'll see, that's all.'

Chapter Nineteen

EDGAR SAID that Yannis was more likely to talk if supplied with something to make his mouth work more smoothly, as he put it, so they took him to a café in the square and furnished him with a generous helping of retsina. Whether he suspected an ulterior motive or not, Yannis was not about to turn down a free drink, and by the time he was halfway down his second glass sure enough his defences were down, and they put the question to him. He was wary at first and denied knowing anything about it, but on being assured that they had no interest in turning him in or getting anybody into trouble for theft, he was at last induced to talk. Yes, it was true that he had been paid by someone at the dig to carry some things across to Turkey. There was a man he met on the other side who took the cargo and gave him the payment. He had done it three or four times—certainly not more. It paid better than carrying cigarettes. He had never looked inside the boxes, because what business was it of his? Only one time his correspondent had opened a crate and taken something out of it, but Yannis could not see what it was because it was wrapped in paper and the man had taken it into another room. It seemed heavy, though, and he thought perhaps it was something made of stone. He had taken the crate back with him because he had a use for it, but had absent-mindedly left it on the boat.

'You ought to be more careful, leaving things like that lying around,' said Edgar. 'Somebody might find you out.'

'An empty crate proves nothing,' replied Yannis.

'You knew they were things from the dig, though?' Angela said.

He made a gesture as though to say it was obvious. Now came the question.

'Who gave you the stuff?' she asked.

He pursed up his lips and toyed with his drink.

'You may as well tell us,' said Edgar, filling up Yannis's glass again.

Yannis remained unwilling.

'Why do you need to know? You told me you were going to keep quiet.'

'About the theft, yes. But this is a matter of murder.'

Yannis stared.

'What? The lady on the beach?'

'Yes. We think she was blackmailing one of the archae-ologists about stolen antiquities.'

'And you're saying Schulz killed her for that?'

'Oh, so it was Schulz, was it?' said Edgar, exchanging glances with Angela as Yannis looked furious with himself for his slip of the tongue.

There was no more to be learned, so they left Yannis to the retsina bottle and came away.

'I was so sure it was the professor, because of the note,' said Angela. 'I could have sworn it was Schulz who wrote it.'

'Who's to say he didn't? Look at it this way: if Cavell

suspected Schulz and mentioned it to the professor, surely the prof would have had a word with Schulz directly rather than engaging in all this hole-and-corner stuff with secret notes under the door. After all, he is in charge of the dig. No,' he went on, 'if you ask me your original theory was right: Cavell did suspect Delisi and reported it to Schulz unwittingly, not realizing that he was talking to the thief himself. Schulz saw the game would be up if he didn't do something fast, so he fobbed Cavell off with some excuse about looking into it. I expect he was planning to cover his tracks as quickly as possible.'

'But he didn't need to, because Roy died,' said Angela thoughtfully.

'Very convenient for him. Have we found our murderer, do you think?'

'It looks likely, doesn't it? But the proof's the thing.'

'Yes. We've been knocking our heads against a brick wall with Cavell, but Miss Brinkhurst is another matter. The police might ignore an accident, but they'll be crawling all over the place for a murder. I shouldn't be surprised if they come up with something to connect Schulz to her death before long. Perhaps we won't be needed at all in the end. You won't mind, will you?'

'He was there on the beach yesterday morning when her body was found,' said Angela. 'Was he the one to find it? Was he getting rid of evidence, perhaps?'

'It's a thought.'

'Let's go back to the hotel. I'd like to see whether there's any news.'

As it turned out, the police wanted to speak to Mr. and Mrs. Merivale about the death of Miss Brinkhurst—purely to find out whether there was any information they could offer with regard to the tragedy. The chief of police was particularly interested in the early evening period of Saturday.

'I understand that Lady Trenoweth and Miss Brinkhurst had been to Rhodes for the day, and returned at about five o'clock,' he said. 'Miss Brinkhurst settled Lady Trenoweth for a quick nap before dinner then came into the lounge. At seven Lady Trenoweth wanted her nurse and went to look for her, but she was nowhere to be found. We know Miss Brinkhurst spoke to Mr. Peterson and Mr. Halliday in that two-hour period, but neither of them can tell us where she went after that. Did you happen to see her?'

'No,' replied Angela. 'I hadn't seen her for a day or two. We went into Rhodes ourselves on Saturday but didn't run across them at all. Then we came back and got ready, and went back into Rhodes for the dance.'

'I see.' He wrote something down in laborious Italian.

'Did I hear you've arrested somebody for the murder?' Angela wanted to know.

'That is official business,' he replied, and dismissed them both.

Edgar wanted to have a bath before dinner, so he disappeared upstairs and Angela went out onto the terrace, where she found Philip Halliday busy scribbling in his notebook. She did not wish to disturb him but he glanced up as she came out.

'Why do unpleasant things always give one inspiration?' he said, looking at his notebook in distaste. 'She was a ghastly woman, but she didn't deserve to die, and now I'm full of ideas. Have the Italians given you a grilling yet?'

'Yes. I asked them about the two fishermen they're meant to have arrested, and was well and truly squashed for my pains.'

'Well, I can tell you: they've been released, since it turns out they both have cast-iron alibis.'

'Why wouldn't the police tell *me* that?' said Angela.

He tapped his nose.

'You don't think I found out from the police, do you? No, I went straight to the central source of all news— Kostis, who knows everything.'

'But if it wasn't the fishermen, then who was it?'

'I don't know. The police seem particularly interested in the period before we all went to the dance on Saturday, which is when I saw her. Apparently I was one of the last people to speak to her.'

'Ah yes, the policeman told me *that*, at any rate. I don't suppose she said anything particularly significant?'

'I can't even remember,' he replied ruefully. 'I wanted to go and dress, so I put her off as quickly as I could. It certainly wasn't anything important, though—just some trite observation on the weather, I expect. Then she cornered Peterson, who couldn't get away so easily, although he didn't seem to mind her much.'

Angela sighed inwardly. She supposed she ought to find out what Mr. Peterson knew. She found him in a corner of the lounge, looking pensive. He looked up as she approached.

'I hear they've released those two fishermen,' said Angela by way of preamble.

'Yes,' he replied.

'Have you spoken to the police? Mr. Halliday told me you were the last person to speak to Miss Brinkhurst, so I expect they were very curious to know what she said.'

Of course this was merely a polite way of saying, '*I* am very curious to know what she said.' Luckily Mr. Peterson was only too happy to oblige her.

'Why, yes, they did want to know, and I'm afraid I had

to disappoint them. She asked me if I was going to the dance, and I said yes, and then she said she'd been quite the dancer as a girl but hadn't done it for a long time, then she wished me well of it and went away. There might have been some other remarks but I don't recollect them. If I'd known it would be the last time I'd speak to her I'd have paid more attention.'

He looked subdued, quite unlike his usual ebullient self.

'She was a mighty fine lady, and very kind to me,' he muttered after a pause. 'I only wish things had been different.'

'Different? What do you mean?'

He did not reply. Angela noticed he was rubbing his hands together nervously. At last he burst out unhappily:

'This detective-work: it's not always fun, is it? I mean, it's all very nice snooping about and looking for clues and putting them together and finding the guilty party and getting praise from everybody, but…'

'But what?' said Angela.

'Nothing. It's just—sometimes you find things out about people that you'd rather not have known.'

'What have you found out?'

'She was very kind to me,' he said again, as though he were trying to convince himself of something.

Angela said gently:

'You really ought to speak up if you know anything.'

He sighed.

'Yes, I know. I've been trying to make up my mind to it —it's just that I hate to speak ill of the dead, and this won't do her reputation any good at all.'

Angela resisted the urge to shake it out of him and merely put on her most encouraging look. At last he seemed to make up his mind.

'All right, then, I'll tell you—one detective to another.

You see, I was looking forward to the dance on Saturday, and I was ready a little early, so I went to sit in the reading-room to think awhile. I was in that high-backed chair—you know, the one that faces the window, when I heard someone come in. Two people. They couldn't see me because of the chair, and I was going to make myself known but then they began talking and after that I couldn't say a thing.'

'Who was it?'

'One of them was Miss Brinkhurst, I know that for sure,' he replied. 'The other one was a man. The voice was familiar but they were both speaking so quietly I couldn't quite place it.'

'What were they saying?'

He swallowed.

'It wasn't a nice conversation. There was a lot of pussy-footing around to start with, and she seemed to be drop-ping hints about something. The man was polite, but you could see he had no idea what she was talking about. Then she came right out and said it—she said she'd found out something about him that had surprised her, and she'd never thought he could have done such a thing. Then he asked what she meant but she wouldn't tell him—just kept on saying she'd been so surprised to find it out.'

He looked slightly sick.

'It put me in mind of a cat playing with a mouse. She was playing with him, that's what it was. She sounded so pleased with herself it was obvious she was enjoying it.'

Angela remembered Miss Brinkhurst's sly, complacent expression during their own encounter in the reading-room, and her dismay as the other woman had laid bare her secret. Had she been collecting information on every-body in the hotel?

Peterson went on:

'Finally he said something like, "I've had enough of this. I don't know what you're talking about," and he opened the door, but she said, "Not so fast—I haven't finished yet. Don't you want to know what I found in Mr. Cavell's trunk?"'

Angela looked up, instantly alert. So it *was* Miss Brinkhurst who had searched the trunk. She felt some little satisfaction at having guessed correctly. Mr. Peterson went on:

'He came back in, then she started to talk, but he said, "For heaven's sake, keep your voice down!" I guess you can imagine me sitting there, rooted to the spot, straining to hear. But they were talking so low I missed half of it. It was clear enough that she knew something to his disadvantage. She said something about how it would be terrible for his reputation if the world found out about it, but that he wasn't to worry— she'd keep it quiet, and his secret was quite safe with her.'

'But you have no idea what the secret was?'

He shook his head regretfully.

'They were talking so low I can't be sure.'

Angela pondered, then decided to show her hand.

'I don't suppose it had something to do with the archaeological dig, did it?' she ventured. 'Was there some question of antiquities going missing?'

He stared, then comprehension dawned suddenly across his face.

'It might have—why, yes! Yes, of course! I'd forgotten about that. Yes, there was some mention of the temple, and a statue, and—what else did she say?' He rubbed his chin. 'I only wish I could remember, but I was concentrating so hard on not breathing that I could hardly pay attention to what they were saying. I know she mentioned Cavell.' He looked at her curiously. 'Is there something going on at the dig? What do you know about that? Who has been stealing antiquities?'

'Dr. Schulz,' she replied.

He stared.

'How did you find that out?'

'Never mind, but you must keep it quiet for now.'

'I will,' he promised.

'Was it Dr. Schulz you heard?'

'I guess it must have been,' he replied. 'He was speaking too low for me to hear whether he had a German accent, but now you come to mention it, it certainly did sound very like him.'

'Did she ask him for money?'

'Not as such.' He looked uncomfortable. 'But I won't say I didn't get the idea that that was what she wanted.'

'What did Dr. Schulz say?'

'He tried to bluster it out at first, but he sounded fidgety. He said, "Don't worry, I can explain everything, but please don't say anything here, as someone might come in and get the wrong idea". You can be sure I froze in my seat at that! What if they came over to the window and saw me? It would have been awkward, to say the least. Anyway, he said he'd meet her down on the beach later that evening and explain everything. She said, "Don't forget!" in a playful kind of way, then they went out. Well, you can guess how unpleasant it was to hear all this, as I'd thought of her as such a good woman.' His eyes grew round. 'Say, does that mean Dr. Schulz…'

'It rather looks like it, doesn't it? He didn't come to the dance, so presumably he was here in St. Michael all Saturday night. I'd be interested to know whether he did meet Miss Brinkhurst down on the beach as he said.'

Peterson shook his head.

'It was a bold move on his part. Why, anybody might have seen him!'

'Not really. The light would have been fading by that time, and her body was found behind the rocks. It would have been easy enough for him to do it as long as he acted quickly.'

He gave a shiver.

'I don't like this,' he said.

'You know you'll have to report this to the police, don't you?' said Angela.

'Oh, but Miss Brinkhurst…'

'Never mind that. It's unfortunate the truth will have to come out, but you won't help find her murderer by keeping quiet. This is important evidence.'

'I guess it is.' He fell silent for a few moments. 'I was wrong about Roy Cavell, wasn't I?' he said suddenly. 'It wasn't suicide at all. Dr. Schulz killed him.'

Angela nodded.

'I think it's quite likely. I think he suspected someone had been stealing and told Schulz about it, not realizing Schulz himself was the thief, and Schulz decided to put him out of the way.'

Peterson drew himself up, and began to look much more like his old self.

'Then it's my duty to report it,' he said self-importantly.

Chapter Twenty

BUT DR. SCHULZ was too quick for the police. On Peterson's reporting what he had overheard in the reading-room, they went to look for him and found him alighting from his car, having just returned from the dig. Unfortunately for them, at the first mention of antiquities he jumped straight back into the car and departed with all speed, and by the time the police had gone to give chase it was too late: he had had plenty of time to get away. Whatever suspicions the police had had about him had now become certainties, and the investigation now turned to the activities up at the archaeological dig. All this Angela and Edgar learned from Kostis, who was enjoying the uproar immensely despite the continued intrusive presence of the police at the hotel.

'He's skipped, then,' said Edgar. 'Was it something we said?'

'But he was a respected academic,' said Angela. 'Why did he throw it all away and ruin his reputation for a few trinkets and a little bit of money?'

Kostis lowered his voice.

'I do not know that he was so respected. He arrived only four months ago and Professor Delisi did not think anything of him when he first came. He was very exasperated and asked his wife why the Archaeological School had sent him such a third-rate man. There had been some question about one of Dr. Schulz's publications, I think. The professor thought it was not—how do you say it—up to scratch.'

'How on earth do you know that?' asked Angela in surprise.

'I heard him say it myself when I was serving breakfast. Nobody ever takes notice of a waiter,' he explained.

'Oh!' exclaimed Angela, thinking with no little alarm of what she and Edgar might have said to their own disadvantage while Kostis was pouring their coffee. The young man went on:

'But Dr. Schulz did not cause any trouble—at least at first—so the professor did not complain any more. Everybody is complaining now, though,' he finished with some satisfaction.

'I don't suppose you know where he is?' Angela asked, for it seemed that if anybody would know Kostis would.

Kostis shrugged.

'This is a small island. Where can he go?'

'If he has any sense he'll hop straight on a boat, get to Smyrna or Cyprus as quickly as he can, and then disappear,' observed Edgar.

'I think he will not get that far,' said Kostis.

———

By the next morning Schulz had still not been found, but most of the police had departed, much to Mr. Florakis's relief. According to Kostis they had gone up to the dig, since there was some idea that Schulz had gone to ground and was hiding in the fortress. There was no sense in hanging about the hotel waiting for news, and in any case the sun was shimmering invitingly on the water, so Angela and Edgar decided to go for a stroll along the cliff path.

'They might listen to you now about Cavell,' said Edgar as they walked.

'I doubt it—unless Schulz confesses to everything or they find some conclusive proof that he was responsible for Roy's death. I'd still like to know where the missing suitcase has got to, though.'

'It might be in Schulz's room.'

'I thought of that, but it's not. I went there before we came out and asked the maid, and she said she'd never seen any such thing there.'

'How did you know which room he was in?'

'I looked at the hotel register when Mr. Florakis's back was turned, of course.'

'Of course. Well, then, I imagine it's gone into the sea, as we suggested before. In that case we'll never find it, unless it washes up somewhere.'

Angela wrinkled her nose.

'It's been an unsatisfactory sort of investigation altogether,' she said.

'You can't always expect black and white answers. You may just have to accept that we'll never know for certain what happened to Roy Cavell.'

Angela was forced to admit the truth of that, but still she was not happy.

They were just then surprised by a mountain-goat which sprang up suddenly onto the path in front of them, seemingly from nowhere. It glared at them balefully then went off to chew some twigs.

'How *do* they do that?' said Angela.

She went to peer over the edge of the cliff. Another goat looked up at her curiously from six feet below, attached by some mysterious force to the almost vertical cliff face. It twitched its ears at her then turned its attention back to a patch of vegetation that was growing out of a crevice.

'What's that?' said Angela suddenly.

Edgar joined her to look. Something was caught among the branches of the plant on which the goat was feasting. It was a piece of paper, creased and folded and torn. Even from where they stood they could see there was handwriting on it. The goat spotted the paper and nibbled experimentally at it.

'Hi! Don't eat it!'

Angela flapped a hand, startling the goat, which sprang indignantly up the cliff in two bounds then went to join its fellow and squabble gently over some juicy leaves. They stared at the paper as it fluttered tantalizingly out of reach.

'Well! No wonder we didn't find it the other night,' said Angela.

She gazed speculatively at Edgar, whose face took on a wary expression.

'What are you looking at me like that for? Don't tell me you're thinking of sending me down there.'

'Oh, but surely it must be the rest of the letter from the Savoy! It's not more than a few feet down. I'm sure you could get it quite easily.'

He stared at the paper with disfavour.

'This rock is practically perpendicular,' he pointed out.

'That goat managed it.'

'In case you hadn't noticed, I'm not a goat.'

'I bet you'd do it for Sophia Delisi.'

'I would *not* do it for Sophia Delisi.' He deliberated, then sighed. 'I will do it for you, though, if you insist.'

She beamed at him.

'I knew you would. How splendid! Now, how do we go about it?' She cast about, looking for possible hand-holds. 'This bush is almost on the edge and reasonably firmly rooted. Could you hold on to that and reach it, do you think?'

'Not without adding an extra two feet to the length of my arms.'

'Well, then, what if I lie close to the edge and hang on to you?'

'Hardly—if I fall I'll pull you over with me, and there's no sense in us both taking a header into the ocean.' He eyed the bush, judging the distance between it and the paper caught in the branches below. 'There's nothing else for it—I shall have to climb down. I wish we had a length of rope, but since we don't my belt will have to do.'

He removed the article in question and fastened it tightly around the base of the bush.

'Not as solid as I'd like,' he said, tugging on it, 'but I dare say it will hold.' He took off his jacket. 'You'd better kiss me goodbye, just in case.'

'You might be a *little* more optimistic,' she said, but did it anyway.

Taking the loose end of the belt in his hand, he lay flat and edged himself backwards until his legs were over the edge.

'This is doing my clothes no good at all,' he remarked. 'Well, here goes. Farewell, sweet lady. Remember me fondly in the years to come.'

'Don't!' exclaimed Angela.

He smirked and saluted her ironically, then lowered himself down carefully. She knelt and held tight onto the belt in case it gave way, more to feel as though she were doing *something* to help, than for any good it might do. His head disappeared below the edge and she peeped over in trepidation.

'It's not too bad,' he said from a little way below. 'There are plenty of footholds. Now, how to reach it...'

He stretched out a hand. There was nothing between him and the water eighty feet below, and only a thin strap of leather preventing him from plummeting to his doom. Angela shut her eyes.

'Got it!' he said triumphantly.

In a trice he was back up on solid ground, brandishing his prize and looking immensely pleased with himself. Angela clapped her hands together.

'Darling!'

'Darling indeed. Do I get another kiss?'

'You most certainly do,' said Angela fervently, suiting the action to the word. He retrieved his belt and jacket and brushed himself down as best he could, then they put their heads together to look at the letter. It was weathered and torn, and showed unmistakable signs of goat attention, for a good chunk of it was missing from one side, but the writing was still legible enough.

'It *is* the Savoy,' said Edgar. 'I knew I recognized it.'

The letter was dated the 20th of May, and read as follows:

Dear Roy,

I told you I'd come to Europe at last and so I have! It was time I took a vacation and you know I like to do things properly, so I'm doing the full tour of Europe—Paris, Rome, Naples, Greece—the whole continent, if I can fit it into two months. I'll tell you everything later, but I have to get this letter off in a hurry because I'm leaving for Paris tomorrow and I want to make sure it arrives on time.

Now here's a surprise for you—I'm going to take a few days out of my vacation to come to Rhodes and talk about that job of yours. If I can't persuade you in person to … give it up altogether. I'll be arriving on the 15th June at … oking forward to seeing Esther again. When's the wedding? Don't tell me you already got married.

So long, and I'll see you on the 15th!

Bill

Angela stared at the torn piece of paper in her hand.

'The 15th of June. That's the day before we arrived—the day Cavell died, in fact.' She remembered something. 'Of course—I'd forgotten Esther told me Bill was coming to see Roy in person, but she never said when. But where is this Bill? Did he come here? What does it all mean?'

'I've no idea.'

She put the letter in her pocket.

'Let's go back. I want to speak to Esther and see what she can tell us about this mysterious friend of Roy's.'

'Do you think he's important?'

'He's a loose end,' she replied. 'He might mean nothing, but I'd like to know where he is now.'

'Perhaps he changed his mind and didn't come at all.'

'Perhaps. Perhaps he came a week early and met Roy, then left.' She eyed him sideways. 'Or perhaps he came, pushed his friend into the sea and is still here somewhere.'

'Did he strangle Miss Brinkhurst too, then?'

'Anybody might have strangled her,' replied Angela. 'I might have done it myself if she'd provoked me enough. But we do have evidence that she was blackmailing Dr. Schulz, so at present I have no reason to doubt he's the one who did it.'

'In that case, what you're suggesting is that the two deaths were completely separate crimes. Rather a big coincidence, don't you think? And why would Bill come all the way to Rhodes to murder his friend?'

'There you have me. I agree that Bill is most likely a distraction, but I'd like to find out more about him all the same, if only to cross him off my list.'

Back at the hotel Edgar went off to change out of his grubby things, and Angela went to inquire for Miss Grayson. Fortunately for her, Esther was not at work that day, for the events up at the dig had caused such an upset that Professor Delisi had far too many other things on his mind to worry about what his assistant was doing. Angela found Miss Grayson sitting with Lady Trenoweth in the lounge, reading aloud to her.

'What can you tell me about Roy's friend Bill?' Angela asked.

Esther looked surprised.

'What do you want to know?'

'To start with, what's his full name? William something, I assume.'

'No, his name's Jack—Jack Billings, but he always went by Bill.'

'Billings?' Angela frowned. Where had she seen that name before? 'Do you know him well?'

'A little. He and Roy were great friends at college but I haven't seen him in a long time.'

'How long?'

'I don't remember—I guess it must be eight years ago or more. Why?'

'You told me Roy received a letter from him that said he intended to come out to Rhodes.'

'So I did.'

'When was he supposed to arrive?'

'I don't know—oh!' she paused. 'Yes I do, of course I do. He was meant to come on the day Roy went to Athens. He said so in the letter. That's why Roy didn't want to go —because he'd miss Bill.' Her face fell. 'One of the reasons, anyway.'

'Did he turn up in the end?'

'No, not that I know of.' She frowned. 'I wonder why.'

'Perhaps Roy telegraphed to put him off, or to arrange to meet him in Athens instead.'

'That's possible. But if he did, he didn't tell me. You'd be better off asking *her* about that.'

Angela did not need to ask whom she meant by 'her.'

'I think we were about to begin chapter twelve,' said Lady Trenoweth pointedly.

'Are you sure Bill didn't come to Rhodes?' asked Angela, ignoring her. 'I mean, would you recognize him if you did see him?'

'Why yes, of course I'd recognize him,' replied Esther.

'What did he look like?'

Esther considered.

'Kind of nondescript, I guess you'd say. Pleasant enough to look at, but nothing you'd notice in particular.'

'Was he tall or short?'

'Middling height, perhaps,' hazarded Esther. She seemed to realize this was not much use. 'I'm sorry, but I'm not very good at describing people, and there wasn't much that stood out about him.'

Angela tried again.

'Are you sure you haven't seen him here on Rhodes at all?'

'Quite sure.'

'People do change in the space of eight years, you know,' Angela insisted, but Esther was firm. She had met Jack Billings quite enough times to know him by sight, and would certainly have recognized him had she seen him here on the island.

Angela retired, defeated. Next, she went in search of Sophia Delisi, who was sunning herself by the pool. Mrs. Delisi could not tell her much except to say that Roy had told her of his determination to speak to Bill about a job on the day he was supposed to go to Athens. She had not been terribly interested in Bill, for she had had no intention of going anywhere with Roy, so she had not inquired further, and had no idea whether or not Bill had ever turned up.

Dissatisfied, Angela withdrew. She appeared to have reached a dead end with regard to the mysterious Bill, for since nobody had seen him it looked as though he had changed his mind about coming to Rhodes after all. That meant he had had nothing to do with the deaths of Roy Cavell or Miss Brinkhurst, and so Dr. Schulz must be their man. All she could do now was wait until they caught him.

Chapter Twenty-One

THE DAY PASSED with no sign of Dr. Schulz. After tea Edgar wanted to go and see Georgios again.

'I don't suppose you want to come, do you?' he said doubtfully. 'Rather a bore for you.'

'Yes, I'll come,' replied Angela. Of course she wanted to come. Not because she wanted to keep an eye on her husband and make sure he was not tempted to fall into bad company or anything of that sort; no, she was merely doing a sick old man a good turn by paying him a visit.

Georgios was still in bed when they arrived.

'You here again,' he wheezed. 'What's all the goings-on at the hotel I hear about? Kostis says they know who killed the big Englishwoman.'

'They think it was Dr. Schulz,' said Angela. 'Miss Brinkhurst found out he was stealing things from the dig, you see.'

Georgios waved a hand.

'Pfft. Everybody knew he was stealing things from the dig.'

'*You* obviously did, you old reprobate,' said Edgar. 'I suppose Yannis told you.'

The old man cackled.

'Yannis! What did you give Yannis yesterday? He didn't wake up until two, and when he came downstairs he looked like a big dog chewed him up and spat him out.'

'We didn't give him enough to do that,' replied Edgar. 'He must have kept on drinking after we left him.'

'You should stop drinking, I tell him. You drink and you get the Eyeties after you.' He scowled. 'I try to teach him my old tricks but he don't want to know. Kostis, now, he has the head and the eye for the jewels, but he's too straight. You ask me, he'll get married and end up running that hotel.'

He shook his head at the disappointment his two sons had caused him.

'Did Yannis warn Dr. Schulz yesterday?' said Angela suddenly. 'Schulz drove off as soon as he saw the police, but why should he have taken fright like that if he hadn't known they were coming after him?'

Georgios shrugged.

'I don't know. And why do you care?'

'Angela rather fancies herself as a detective,' replied Edgar slyly. 'She wants to run him to ground and present him to the police in a blaze of glory.'

'You beast—I never said anything of the sort!' said Angela indignantly.

'You'd like to, though, wouldn't you?'

Georgios gave his wheezing laugh.

'Just you keep your pretty nose out of it—he's probably well off the island by now and halfway to Athens and then they'll never find them. Better go back to the hotel and enjoy the rest of your holiday.'

There came a sudden thump from upstairs. Angela glanced up.

'Is that Yannis?'

'Yes,' replied Georgios. 'Still sleeping it off. He's going out fishing tonight so he needs to be fresh.'

Angela would have believed him, except that as soon as the words had come out of her mouth she had suddenly remembered catching sight of Yannis in the distance on their way here, walking down towards the harbour. She looked up sharply and was just in time to see a glance of understanding between Edgar and Georgios. Realization dawned.

'He's here, isn't he?' she said incredulously. 'You're hiding Dr. Schulz upstairs.'

Georgios said nothing, but his face assumed an innocent expression which merely had the effect of making him look supremely guilty.

'Edgar?' she inquired, turning to her husband.

'I promise you I didn't know. What's this all about, Georgios?'

Georgios made a gesture to indicate that none of this was anything to do with him. Angela was still looking accusingly at Edgar.

'Look, I swear I had no idea. D'you think I'd have brought you here if I'd known and wanted to keep it secret from you?' he demanded.

This was a fair point. Angela bit back the remark she had been about to make and subsided. Edgar grimaced.

'We'd better fetch him out then, hadn't we, now he's given himself away. He's not likely to brandish a gun at us, is he?' he asked of Georgios.

'What, that sissy? He's strictly an amateur.'

Edgar and Angela were already halfway up the stairs. At the top was a dingy room with an unmade bed on which Dr. Schulz was sitting. He started violently when he saw them and swore in German.

'Ach, you did not bring the police, did you?'

'As it happens, we didn't,' replied Edgar. 'What the devil are you doing here?'

'Waiting for Yannis to come back and take him off the island once it gets dark, I imagine,' said Angela. 'That's right, isn't it? But why didn't you go last night?'

Edgar began to laugh.

'I rather fear that was our fault for plying Yannis with retsina and rendering him drunk and incapable. Dear me, have you been hiding here all day, Schulz?'

Schulz looked at them mutinously but made no reply.

'You were bound to get caught sooner or later, you know,' said Edgar. 'There's only so long you can fiddle the books before somebody notices. You ought to have stopped before you were found out.'

'Bah—who would have noticed? Delisi thinks of nothing but his own standing, and looking good before the governor and the men in Rome. He took all the best pieces and handed them out like pennies to anyone who asked for them, just so they would call him a great fellow and keep on paying him to grub about in the dirt here on this island at the ends of the earth. He talks in this high way about the museum and his duty to the public, but go and visit the governor and you will see Delisi has given him all the most beautiful objects to put on display in his own private house. If they can take for themselves, then why not I? After all, there is plenty to go around. I found many of the things myself, so why should I not be rewarded?'

'Because they're meant to be for the benefit of every-one,' said Angela.

'What do the public know of these things? Can they distinguish one gold necklace or one broken statue from

another? There are plenty of relics for them to look at—
they will not miss one or two.'

'Roy Cavell did.'

Schulz's face took on a brooding expression.

'Damn him, and that girl of his. They came along and
they liked to make lists. "Are you sure this is right, Doctor?"
he said with savage mimicry. "I can't read what you wrote
here. I think someone has made a mistake." Still, I was
careful, and they could never prove anything. If the police
come I will point to the professor and tell them he is every
bit as bad, even if he was not selling the things he took.
Money is not the only temptation.'

'That won't help you much,' said Edgar. 'The Italians
—including him—have it all sewn up here, and can pretty
much do as they please. And in any case, it's not just theft
they want you for.'

'Ach, yes, Yannis said something, but he was very drunk
so I thought he was saying imbecilities. What else is it they
want of me?'

'They think you murdered Miss Brinkhurst.'

Schulz stared.

'Then it is true. But they don't really mean it, do they?
Why should I have killed that stupid woman?'

'Because she found out what you were doing and tried
to blackmail you,' replied Edgar.

'That is ridiculous,' he said haughtily. 'I hardly spoke to
her. How could she know what I was doing? I deny this
absolutely.'

'Deny it all you like, but you and she were overheard
talking about it in the reading-room, I'm afraid.'

'Who overheard me? When was this?'

'Never mind who, but it was on Saturday evening.'

'Did this person see me? Of course they did not,
because it was not me she spoke to. It must have been

another person, and this is a gross slander against my name.'

'You're hardly in a position to complain about that,' said Edgar dryly.

'What about Roy Cavell?' Angela asked. 'You say you were careful and they couldn't prove anything, but Roy told you his suspicions, didn't he?'

'Ach, yes, it was very inconvenient. Luckily I was able to put him off, but since he was getting too close I decided it would be safer to stop what I was doing for a while until things had died down.'

'Did you kill him?' she asked.

'Cavell? Of course not! That was an accident, yes? Or perhaps he killed himself. Do the police think I murdered Cavell too?'

He finally seemed to realize that he was in trouble, and his face grew alarmed.

'They don't really think that, do they? It's not true, I tell you! Yes, perhaps I took a few things when I should not have, but I never killed anybody.'

'If you want to convince us of that you'd better tell us the whole story,' said Edgar. 'Let's start with Cavell telling you about his suspicions. When was that?'

'I don't know. A day or two before he died. I confess it put me in a fright for a little while. Fortunately for me he thought it was Delisi, but it made me realize that I had been careless and that I must cover my tracks as quickly as possible. I pretended to take his suspicions seriously and promised I would investigate and tell him what I had found out.'

'Then you wrote him a note about it on Monday and put it under his door,' said Angela.

'Yes,' he replied in surprise. 'How do you know?'

'He never received it. It went under the rug and I found it when we moved into his room.'

'Ah, that explains why he did not mention it to me. Yes, I had invented for myself a very nice story. I intended to tell him that Delisi had told me the goods had been shipped in great secrecy to somebody very high up in Rome, who wanted them for his own house, and it was all on the hush-hush, as you say. But I was going to assure him that nothing had been stolen. At any rate, the note was not necessary, because I saw him in the lobby when I returned from the dig on Monday afternoon. He was getting ready to leave for Athens and I wanted to impress upon him the vital importance of saying nothing, and to see whether he believed me, so I told him I was going into Rhodes myself and would take him in my car later.'

'So that's why he dismissed Yannis,' said Angela. 'That explains it. But didn't you go and look for him when he didn't turn up for his lift?'

'He did turn up,' replied the doctor.

'What?'

'Yes. We met at the appointed time and I took him into Rhodes.'

They stared at him in astonishment.

'Good Lord!' exclaimed Edgar. 'Why didn't you say so before? We've all been assuming Cavell never left St. Michael.'

Schulz looked uncomfortable.

'I did not say so because he hinted to me that he had mentioned all this to someone else. I do not know who it was, but imagine my position when he was found dead: if the unknown person had spoken up about Cavell's suspicions and the police had started poking their noses into the case, they might have got the mistaken impression that Cavell had not died accidentally, and then they would have come looking for me. Better stay out of it and pretend I never saw him that day, I told myself. Besides, it did not matter whether he was in Rhodes or St. Michael. Dead is dead, and it was nothing to do with me.'

'Are you sure of that? Didn't you kill him?' asked Edgar.

'Of course not! We drove to Rhodes and I made certain that he did not suspect me of anything, then I left him at the Grand Hotel and never saw him again.'

'Why there and not the governor's house?'

'I don't know. That was where he wanted to go.'

'Did he have a brown leather suitcase with him?' Angela wanted to know.

'He had a small suitcase. It might have been brown leather, but I did not notice.'

'If you left him in Rhodes, then why was he found in St. Michael? Didn't you ever wonder?'

'Maybe. I don't know. I thought perhaps he had too much to drink, fell in at Rhodes and drifted down the coast. I thought it was most likely a coincidence of the current that they found him back here.'

Just then they were interrupted by the sound of the front door bursting open in the lower room, and Yannis came haring up the stairs two at a time.

'The police are on their way!' he announced breathlessly. 'Somebody must have seen you and squealed.'

'I must get out!' exclaimed Schulz in dismay.

He leapt up and made a bee-line for the stairs—but it was too late, for before he was halfway down there came a hammering at the door. Yannis ran to the window and opened it.

'I'm not taking the fall for this,' he said. 'They better not find me here. Tell them I'm out fishing. I'll go out the back way.'

Almost before he had finished speaking he had wriggled out through the window and disappeared up onto the roof. Edgar looked as though he had half a mind to follow him, but thought better of it and remained where he was.

'Well done,' murmured Angela, and had the satisfaction of seeing him look slightly embarrassed.

The police had no intention of waiting to be admitted, and within a few moments the house was full of confusion, with much banging about and talking in four different languages at once. Dr. Schulz was determined not to go without a fight, but he was eventually subdued and carried off, protesting loudly.

'We had no idea he was upstairs,' Angela assured the chief of police. 'We came to visit our sick friend here.'

'He burst into my house this morning and I couldn't get rid of him, your honour,' said Georgios. 'I've never seen him in my life before. I'm an honest man.'

Fortunately, the police were interested only in Dr. Schulz, and so after a brief search of the house they departed.

'Lucky you weren't hiding anything else they might have been interested in,' remarked Edgar to Georgios when they were alone once more.

Georgios patted the bed.

'Under the mattress,' he said with a wink. 'Who wants to lift a sick old man out of bed?'

They took their leave of him, Angela shaking her head, and walked back to the hotel by way of the harbour. Yannis's usual berth was vacant and the sound of a boat engine drifted back towards them from across the water. It appeared he had made good his escape.

'Will they arrest him, do you think?' said Angela.

'Probably. They arrest him about once a week as far as I can tell. They don't usually hold him for more than a day or two, though. As long as Kostis stays out of trouble Georgios ought to be all right. So, then, Cavell made it to Rhodes after all—that's rather a turn-up, isn't it? Or do you think Schulz was lying?'

'I don't see why. We know Cavell had told Philip Halliday of his suspicions—Philip told me so himself—and why should Dr. Schulz have said he gave Cavell a lift when nobody saw them and he might easily have denied it?'

'True enough. Very well, let's assume he's telling the truth. But then why did Cavell come back to St. Michael?'

Angela gave a sudden laugh.

'Why, because he forgot his passport, of course! I thought of it at the very beginning, but it seemed too obvious so I rejected it as a theory. But that must surely be the reason. He put his passport in the wrong trunk by mistake when he was packing, but didn't realize what he'd done until he got to Rhodes, and so had to come back for it. Mr. Peterson thought it meant he never meant to leave at all, but it was much more likely that it was merely an oversight.'

'In that case, how did he get back here? Presumably not in the car with Dr. Schulz, who says he left him at the Grand Hotel and never saw him again. Unless *that* was a lie.'

'No, I think we ought to assume Schulz was telling the truth. If you remember, he seemed awfully surprised at the suggestion that Cavell might have been murdered.'

'Any bad 'un worth his salt can put on a surprised expression.' He looked sideways at her. 'I see you don't rate him as a murderer, though.'

'No, I don't. Oh, I see he has a perfectly good motive, and I won't say he *didn't* do it, but I don't think he took Roy back to the hotel in his car. There's still the question of Bill, you see.'

'Our old friend Bill again,' said Edgar.

'Let's put it together,' went on Angela. 'Remember the letter—why did we find it on the cliff?'

'Because that's where Cavell went into the sea. It must have fallen out of his pocket when he went over.'

'Yes, but why was he carrying the letter with him at all? Take that together with the fact that Dr. Schulz dropped him at the Grand Hotel...'

'Oh, I see,' he said, understanding. 'That's where he was meant to be meeting Bill.'

'Exactly. And of course it makes sense—the Grand Hotel is where everybody stays, and it's almost certainly where a rich young man like Bill would stay when he arrived in Rhodes. We'd have stayed there ourselves if there'd been room. I expect Roy put the letter in his pocket to remind himself of the time of the meeting. As to whether Dr. Schulz took him back to St. Michael, I don't know when Roy realized he'd forgotten his passport, but don't you think he'd go and say hallo to his old friend first before rushing off back to St. Michael, rather than simply not turning up to their meeting? After all, they hadn't seen one another in years, and they only had a few hours before he had to go off to Athens.'

'I see what you mean. So he kept his appointment, then came back to St. Michael by whatever means and here met his doom. But doesn't that mean it was an accident, after all that? We know why he dismissed Yannis now, and we know what the note under the door meant. But I dare say Cavell had a couple of drinks at the Grand Hotel with his pal before he set off back here to fetch his passport. That might easily have caused him to slip and fall in.'

'But why did he decide to go for a walk along the cliff instead of returning immediately to Rhodes? Either to meet his friend again or to go to the governor's house, depending on what time it was? And we *still* don't know where the brown case is.'

'I'd forgotten about that.'

'And most importantly of all, why haven't we heard from Bill?' said Angela. 'Did he stay only one night on Rhodes then go off somewhere else? Where is he now?'

'He might have come on a cruise ship and then gone off the next day.'

'That's a thought. No, that can't be right, though. They only arrive on Saturdays and Tuesdays.' She frowned. 'I wish I knew where Bill was. He's important, I know it.'

'He might still be on the island for all we know.'

'He might, yes. We'll have to ask them at the Grand Hotel.'

'Or is he even at the Hotel Acropolis?' suggested Edgar.

'No. I asked Esther Grayson about that. She knew him years ago and she was quite certain she hadn't seen him there. I asked her several times whether she was sure and she couldn't be budged.'

'Just because she hasn't seen him doesn't mean he's not here. Perhaps he's been hiding in his room and hasn't come out.'

'But why?'

'Because he killed Roy and didn't want anybody to suspect him?'

'If I'd just killed my best friend and nobody knew I was here, the first thing I'd do would be to get off the island,' said Angela practically.

'Perhaps he did, then. Perhaps he whacked Roy on the head, pushed him into the sea then scarpered.'

'Then who tried to kill me?'

'Now *that* might have been Schulz. If Peterson spotted you snooping around that day at the dig, then anybody might have. In fact, I expect everybody did see you but they were all too polite to mention it.'

Angela made a face at him.

'Still,' she said thoughtfully. 'This new information opens up a few possibilities.' She glanced at her watch. 'It's nearly dinner-time, so it's too late to do anything now, but tomorrow we'll go into Rhodes and speak to the people at the Grand Hotel.'

'Yes—with any luck they'll be able to tell us something about what happened that evening. We might search for a taxi-driver too. After all, somebody must have brought Cavell back to St. Michael.'

'Of course, you're right. That's another line of inquiry.' She looked at him eagerly. 'We're close to the solution, I can feel it! We'll go to the Grand Hotel tomorrow, get them to tell us what happened that night and solve the mystery of Roy Cavell's death once and for all.'

'I admire your certainty,' said Edgar.

Chapter Twenty-Two

THE NEXT MORNING they went into Rhodes bright and early, eager to speak to the people at the Grand Hotel and find out whether a Jack Billings had stayed at the hotel on the night of Monday the 15th of June. The manager with whom they spoke was busy and distant, and was not inclined to give them the private information of his guests, or even confirm whether anybody of that name had ever stayed with them. No, he regretted he could not allow them to look at the hotel register. Angela tried everything she could think of to persuade him, but that merely caused him to regard them with increasing suspicion. There was certainly no use in asking him to put out a message to all the taxi-drivers who operated at the hotel, so they came away.

'Bother,' said Angela. 'I did so hope we'd have all the answers by lunch-time. Now what?'

'We'll just have to go and find the taxi-driver ourselves,' said Edgar.

The Grand Hotel had several drivers, of whom they could find only one at that hour, since the ferry traffic had long since died down. He was dozing in his cab out at the front of the hotel and did not appreciate being woken up —especially when he found out that they did not want to hire him. He gave them short shrift in broken English and they retired, crushed.

'Well, that wasn't very polite,' said Angela. 'What shall we do now?'

'Suppose we go and have coffee,' suggested Edgar. 'One of the waiters might remember something about that night.'

This seemed as good an idea as any, so they went back inside and seated themselves. Coffee was served and Angela essayed one or two tentative questions of the waiter, but soon found out that her quest was unlikely to be successful. The waiter had been working on the night in question, but he could not possibly remember who he had served. The hotel was a big one, and constantly very busy. Angela mentioned the name of Jack Billings. He thought he remembered the name, but madam was to understand that he heard so many names and saw so many faces that it was not likely he would recall one person out of hundreds or thousands, especially if this gentleman did not stay at the hotel for very long. It might even have been a different name he remembered. One English name was much like another. He regretted he could not be of any help.

'It's a pity this hotel is so big and popular,' said Angela, when the waiter had gone off. 'Now what shall we do?' She pondered for a moment, then brightened. 'The brown suit-case! Dr. Schulz said he saw Cavell with it. I wonder if he left it here.'

She was not very hopeful that they could get any of the porters to talk, but fortunately they found one who was rendered amenable by the application of hard cash. He went off in search of the suitcase, but returned shaking his head. No such article had been left at the hotel. Angela made a rueful face.

'This has been a useless outing all round. I suppose there's nothing left for us to do.'

'Well, we've come all the way here now, so we may as well go and enjoy ourselves,' replied Edgar.

They spent the day wandering around the town, then returned to the Hotel Acropolis. Angela had not slept well the night before, so she went to lie down while Edgar went to take a dip in the pool.

It had been a most frustrating day: just when she had thought all the answers were within her grasp, they had slipped out of her hands once again. She was now more sure than ever that the elusive Bill was the key to the mystery, but where was he? He was not here at the Hotel Acropolis but he had almost certainly stayed at the Grand Hotel on the night of Monday the 15th. Had he left the island after that? That seemed a reasonable conclusion—after all, if he had remained on Rhodes surely he would have turned up in St. Michael or at the dig sooner or later, if only to see Esther Grayson. On the night they met, Cavell must have mentioned he was going to Athens, so if Bill had no interest in staying on Rhodes he might well have departed the next day without ever finding out that his friend had died on Monday night. Had he met Roy that evening and talked over old times with him? Had they been together for the whole evening, or had Cavell made his excuses and said he could stay only a little while because he had forgotten his passport?

His passport…his passport…now, what was it about passports? One needed a passport to stay at the Grand Hotel, and to swim in the pool. Kostis would not let her swim until she showed him her passport, but she had lost it. Fortunately, the head of a statue of Helios would do instead. She kept it in a new suitcase in smart brown leather she had bought in Athens. She would go and fetch it immediately.

Her room was at the very top of a long flight of stairs, but she must climb it if she wanted to swim in the pool. She climbed and climbed until she was quite out of breath, but the further she ascended the further away her room retreated. At last, with a supreme effort, she reached the top of the stairs and went into her room. Miss Brinkhurst was there, waiting for her, wearing that knowing smile of hers. 'I know who you are,' she said, but Angela was in too much of a hurry to stop and speak to her. She wanted to go into the pool and ask Roy Cavell what had happened to his passport. She brought out her suitcase, opened it, and saw inside, not a statue's head but—

'Goodness!' she exclaimed as she started awake.

The dream had been most disturbing and quite real. She lay there blinking for a minute or two, then got up and went to wash her face, feeling unpleasantly heavy-headed. Perhaps a cup of tea would refresh her. She would go down to the dining-room in a minute, once she had hung up those few clothes she had left on the chair. Edgar's side of the room was much tidier than hers—one did not successfully elude the police for more than ten years by leaving one's things all over the place like a trail of bread-crumbs, she supposed. She really ought to take a leaf out of his book and make the effort to keep things neat, since Marthe was not here to do it for her.

On the floor was the copy of the *Times* she had taken from the reading-room the other day and forgotten to return. She took it and opened it. She had sold most of her business interests some time ago, but had never quite got out of the habit of reading the stock pages—although as Miss Brinkhurst had said, they were sadly out of date and of little use by the time they arrived on Rhodes. She glanced at the prices and then turned to the news to find out what had been going on at home—by which she meant England, of course, although she had not set foot in the country in nearly two years. Perhaps it was time to return, just for a visit, and see how everybody was getting on. She had correspondents, naturally, but letters were no substitute for seeing people in person.

She turned a page and read the headlines. One mentioned the Duke of Irmston, and she thought again of Miss Brinkhurst, who had been interested in the gossip pages. Such a ghoulish woman, she had been. But she was gone now, and it was better not to think ill of the dead; no doubt she had had many good points to balance the bad ones. Angela's eyes scanned the rest of the page and came to a sudden stop as a particular word arrested her attention. She stopped and read the story more closely, then turned to look at the date on the front page of the paper.

'Odd,' she thought, and frowned.

It was probably a coincidence. Still, it was an intriguing one, and she was curious to know more. She went downstairs to return the newspaper to the reading-room. A new guest was sitting in there, an elderly man of the military type, smoking a pipe and harrumphing over the latest edition of the *Daily Telegraph*. He made one or two attempts to engage her in conversation about the dire state of the world, then went back to his paper.

Angela went to rummage through the old newspapers, hoping that the ones from last week were still there. When was it that she had spoken to Miss Brinkhurst? And which were the latest editions of the *Clarion* and the *Herald* on that day? She picked a copy of the *Herald* at random and looked through it, with no result. With a sigh she sat down and set herself to searching through all the newspapers, and at last found what she was seeking in the third copy of the *Clarion* she picked up. She read it, then took the *Herald* of the same date and read that too. At last she threw it down and stared into space. *Was* it a coincidence? *Was* there a connection between what she had just read and all the mysteries here on this far-away island? The only difficulty was that although Bill was the key to it all, he was not here in St. Michael: Esther Grayson had been sure of it, and there was no reason to suppose she was mistaken. Appearances did change over time, but surely not so much as all that? Esther might have overlooked a much-changed Bill by accident if she had not been expecting to see him, but Angela had asked her about him specifically. Surely if he were here Esther would have identified him sooner or later.

What did it mean? And if it was not a coincidence, then how did it fit in here? Angela sighed. If only the manager of the Grand Hotel had allowed them to look through the hotel register. Had she known about Bill earlier she might have taken the opportunity to ask at the desk on the night of the dance, when perhaps she might have found someone more amenable and willing to help her.

The hotel register. She stopped, as a sudden memory came into her head, followed by another, and another. A ridiculous idea began to dawn in her mind. She stared down at the newspaper in her hand as everything began to slot into place. *Was* it so ridiculous? It was an extraordinary idea, but was it too implausible to be true?

'It would certainly explain why Esther didn't recognize him,' she said aloud.

'Eh? What's that?' said the elderly colonel.

Angela apologized and left the reading-room, carrying the copies of the *Herald* and the *Clarion*. Edgar had returned from his swim when she got back to their room, and was lying on the bed comfortably, smoking one of his Turkish cigarettes.

'Where did you get to? I thought you were supposed to be having a nap,' he said.

She sat down on the bed next to him.

'Edgar, I rather think I've been the most awful idiot,' she said.

This of course needed an explanation, which she duly provided with the help of the newspapers. Edgar was gratifyingly astonished at her story.

'My word, I think you could be on to something!' he exclaimed.

'Do you think so? I'm so pleased. I know it sounds terribly far-fetched, but from the evidence we have it could be true, couldn't it? Of course, there are lots of things that still need clearing up, but now we have an idea of what happened it ought to be easier to find proof of what we know—or suspect we know.'

'Yes, the proof's the thing,' agreed Edgar. 'We need to find the missing suitcase, and whatever Miss Brinkhurst stole from Cavell's trunk. I assume she found something in there, otherwise how did she blackmail the murderer?'

Angela made an impatient noise.

'I really was stupid about Miss Brinkhurst. That will teach me to get carried away by an idea.'

'Well, it can't be helped. I suppose we'll find whatever she took and the suitcase in the same place—always assuming they haven't been destroyed. I must say, if someone had been blackmailing me and I'd murdered them then I'd have taken good care to get rid of all the evidence. If our killer has done the same we'll never prove anything.'

'Not everybody is as careful as you are,' observed

Angela. 'I was thinking about that earlier when I noticed how tidy you are. Our murderer isn't a professional criminal, so there's a good chance there are some clues lying around. And even if there aren't, I'm sure there must be evidence elsewhere. It's just a question of whether we can get hold of it in time.' She pondered. 'I might telegraph to New York, or—I know! I'll wire Freddy at the *Clarion*. He ought to be able to find out what we want to know. I'll do it now.'

'Watch your step,' said Edgar as she jumped up and prepared to go out. 'Remember our murderer has killed more than once and won't hesitate to kill again.'

'Don't worry, I'll be careful,' she promised.

———

ANGELA WAS a little late for dinner and found Edgar already seated when she arrived in the dining-room. He looked up from the menu as she took her seat.

'All done?' he asked.

'Yes, I spoke to the chief of police. He took some convincing, but I managed it at last. He's going to send a couple of men over to the hotel to search everybody's rooms first thing tomorrow morning. They want to catch all the guests by surprise so our killer doesn't have time to get rid of it.'

Edgar threw a warning look at Angela—too late, for they had been overheard.

'I beg your pardon, what's that?' said Mr. Peterson at the next table. 'What are they searching for? Is this something to do with the case? I thought it had been closed. Dr. Schulz is behind bars, after all.'

Angela hesitated and glanced at her husband, who shook his head almost imperceptibly.

'I don't believe Dr. Schulz is our murderer,' she said reluctantly at last.

'Oh? Why not?' Peterson wanted to know.

'Because nothing fits. We spoke to him last night just before he was arrested, you see. He says he took Cavell into Rhodes on the night he died and left him there. But if Schulz killed Roy why should he mention having been the last person to see him, when it was only likely to get him into more trouble? Nobody knew about it, so he might easily have kept quiet. There was no need at all for him to tell me about having given Roy a lift, but he did it quite voluntarily.'

Peterson appeared struck by the news.

'He took Cavell into Rhodes, did he? Are you sure of that?'

'Quite sure. So you see, we've been getting it all wrong. We thought Roy never left St. Michael, but in fact he went to Rhodes as he originally intended to, then returned here later on—most likely because he'd forgotten his passport. That seems the most probable explanation, at any rate.'

She threw another glance at Edgar, who gave a resigned shrug.

'We've found out another thing,' she went on. 'He was supposed to be meeting a friend of his—a man called Bill —on the night he died.'

Peterson gaped.

'He was meeting someone? How do you know that?'

'We found a letter Bill sent from London, mentioning that he'd be in Rhodes on the 15th of June. It looks as though it must have fallen out of Cavell's pocket on the cliff top.'

'But who is this Bill? Is he here?'

Peterson looked around eagerly, as though he thought

Bill might be hiding behind a pillar listening to their conversation.

'I don't know where he is,' replied Angela. 'I expect he's left the island by now, but if we can find him he might have some information to give. In the meantime, there's the question of the suitcase Cavell intended to take to Athens with him. It's missing.'

'Maybe he left it at the Grand Hotel if he went into Rhodes as you say.'

Angela regarded him curiously.

'We inquired about that, and he didn't. I think the murderer took it so it wouldn't be found as evidence. Whether he kept it or got rid of it I don't know, but we need to find it if at all possible. When we find the suitcase we'll have found our murderer.'

'That's easier said than done,' said Peterson.

'Well, of course, I can't go searching everyone's rooms, but the police certainly can. That's where I've been— speaking to the police.'

Peterson stared at her, open-mouthed.

'Well! I had no idea of all this! You mean to say you've been keeping these clues a secret from me all this time?'

'It wasn't deliberate,' lied Angela. 'I didn't think to mention it, that's all.'

'But what about Miss Brinkhurst? Who killed her?'

'Not Dr. Schulz, at any rate.'

Peterson looked a little petulant.

'I know what I heard,' he said. 'She was threatening him.'

Angela forbore to point out that he had not been able to identify Dr. Schulz as the speaker until she herself had suggested it to him, for that had been a huge mistake on her part and she did not wish to draw attention to it just now.

Peterson was brooding over what she had told him.

'If you'll pardon my bluntness, I think you're wrong,' he announced at last.

'You still believe Dr. Schulz murdered Cavell and Miss Brinkhurst?'

'Yes, I do. Why, all the evidence points to it! After all, we know he was stealing the antiquities. Mark my words— Cavell and Miss Brinkhurst found out what he was up to and he put them both out of the way with no more thought than he would give to squashing a cockroach.' He stood up and wagged a finger. 'Dr. Schulz did it and I'll prove it!'

He departed, stopping to talk to Lady Trenoweth on his way out.

'He does like to listen in on other people's conversations,' remarked Angela.

'You gave rather a lot away,' said Edgar.

'I did, didn't I? But he says he's going to prove Dr. Schulz did it. Have I ruined everything, do you think?'

'We'll soon find out,' he said.

Chapter Twenty-Three

IT WAS JUST AFTER MIDNIGHT, and the waning moon was bright in the sky when a man came out of the Hotel Acropolis and set off along the road towards the cliff path. He was carrying a small suitcase and appeared to have a purpose in mind. He walked fast, panting slightly with the effort, until he reached the point on the path where the sea came close to the cliff, not far from where Roy Cavell had gone into the water. When he stopped to fetch his breath he heard the sound of footsteps approaching behind him, and turned to see the figure of a woman coming towards him along the path. As she drew nearer he recognized her as Mrs. Merivale.

'Hallo again, Mr. Peterson,' said Angela cheerfully. 'It's late, isn't it? Couldn't you sleep either? I always find a brisk walk helps when I can't drift off.' She caught sight of the suitcase and stared at it in astonishment. 'Goodness me! That's not Roy Cavell's suitcase, is it? You've found it! How clever of you. I'd been looking for it for days. Where was it?'

A guilty expression crossed his face and was replaced by a rueful one.

'I guess you caught me out all right,' he replied wryly. 'I didn't set too much store by what you said about the Cavell case at first, but I was sure Dr. Schulz was our killer so I thought it couldn't do any harm to search his room, and there it was. I found it right away under his bed.'

'How odd. I asked the maid and she said she'd never seen it there. Either she was fibbing or she hasn't been cleaning properly,' she said humorously. 'But why have you brought it out here?'

He looked even more shame-faced.

'I wanted to crack the case myself and didn't want you muscling in on it. So I thought I'd take it far away from the hotel where nobody would see.'

'Well, it doesn't matter. All that matters is that it's found. This is your win and I won't try and steal your thunder.' She glanced at the case again. 'I'm dying to find out whether it really did belong to Roy Cavell. Why don't you open it and see what's inside?'

'I guess I could,' he replied doubtfully.

'Shouldn't you rather take it back to the hotel?' On seeing him look reluctant, she went on, 'Never mind, here will do.'

He hesitated, then put the suitcase down on the ground and crouched down to open it. She watched from a short distance away as he rifled through it unenthusiastically.

'Just clothes,' he said. Then he started and let out an excited exclamation. 'Gracious me! Well if that doesn't beat all!' He glanced up. 'Come here and look at this!'

Angela briefly surveyed the loose rocks that lay on the ground close to where he was.

'I won't, if you don't mind,' she replied. 'I'll stand back here.'

He stared at her for a moment, then turned thought-fully back to the case.

'How did you know about the Grand Hotel, by the way?' asked Angela.

'What?'

'You told me you thought Roy might have left his suit-case at the Grand Hotel. But I never mentioned that he'd been there. I just said that Dr. Schulz had given him a lift into Rhodes.'

Peterson opened and closed his mouth once or twice.

'Well, where else would he go?' he said at last. 'I mean, if he was meeting a friend. Everybody goes to the Grand Hotel.'

'So they do. You stayed there, didn't you?'

'What? No I didn't.'

'Oh, I beg your pardon, I thought you did. You told me how nice the bedrooms were while we were dancing the other night—don't you remember? I expect that's where I got the idea.'

'I—er—did I? Yes—yes, I'm sorry, my mistake. I thought you were asking whether I'd stayed a long time, but it was just the one night—the night before I came to St. Michael.'

'That's rather a coincidence, isn't it? I mean to say, that must have been the same night Roy Cavell came to the Grand Hotel, shortly before he died. I don't suppose you saw him while you were there, did you?'

'Of course I didn't—at least, not as far as I know. Why, I'd never even heard of him until the day after I arrived in St. Michael and found him dead on the beach.' His brow lowered. 'Look, just what exactly are you getting at? Say it straight out, won't you? What are you trying to imply?'

'Very well, then, I'll tell you. Let's start with Cavell's friend Bill. I've been puzzled about Bill ever since I heard he'd written to Roy about giving him a job. But it wasn't until we found the letter he sent from London that I discovered he was meant to be coming here on the 15th of June and realized how important he was to solving the mystery.'

'Why's that?' he asked, almost unwillingly.

'Because we hadn't seen sight or sound of him even though his friend was dead. Had he left the island? But why would somebody make a journey of several days all the way from London to Rhodes for the sake of only a few hours? He was coming because he wanted to persuade Cavell to work for him. If Cavell hadn't been going away presumably Bill would have remained on Rhodes a few days—but Roy died, and after that we couldn't seem to find out what had become of Bill at all. The people at the Grand Hotel weren't very helpful, but Esther Grayson was quite certain she hadn't seen him. She might have missed him had he stayed in Rhodes, but she was sure she hadn't seen him here in St. Michael. So for a while I assumed that either he didn't turn up at all, or that he turned up, met Roy and went off again the next day without ever finding out that his friend had died.'

She eyed Peterson and went on:

'There was a third possibility, though: that he came here, met Roy Cavell and murdered him. I couldn't think why he'd do that, but the facts said it might be possible. The only problem with that, again, was Esther. She'd known Bill a few years ago, so I had to believe her when she insisted she hadn't seen him here. I did wonder whether he mightn't have come to St. Michael and lain low after he killed Cavell, but why on earth would he do that? And besides, I quickly came up against the problem of Miss Brinkhurst. *Somebody* killed her, and as you found out yourself, she had a taste for blackmail. How could she possibly have known about Bill's existence and blackmailed him if he was lying low?'

'I told you it was Dr. Schulz I heard talking to her in the reading-room.'

'No—it was I who told *you* that,' she said. 'And what a fool I was for doing it, all because I suspected Dr. Schulz was the murderer! I gave you an opening and you seized it with both hands. Leaving that aside, I rejected Bill as a possibility since I was sure he would have shown his face sooner or later had he been on the island. But then I remembered something I'd completely overlooked at first.'

'Go on,' he said as she paused.

'Yesterday I wanted to find out where Dr. Schulz's room was—to see if I could get in and search for that suitcase, as it happens—so I sneaked a quick look at the hotel register when nobody was at the desk. And I saw lots of names, including yours.'

Peterson made a sudden move, but thought better of it. Angela maintained her distance and did not take her eyes off him.

'It didn't sink in at the time as I was looking for something else. Very remiss of me not to make the connection immediately, though. According to the hotel register your full name is John Billings Peterson. Cavell's friend was known as Bill, short for Jack—presumably John—Billings. Strange, isn't it? On the one hand we have a missing Jack Billings, and on the other we have a very much present John Billings Peterson. Do you suppose there's a connection?'

He licked his lips.

'I'm not Bill,' he said.

'I know you're not. And I know you're not John Peterson either.'

'That's a lie!' he said sharply. '*I am* John Peterson, and I can prove it! Why, I have a passport and letters from the bank, and anything else you could possibly ask for. I'll show you them when we get back to the hotel. I am Peterson, I tell you!'

Angela shook her head as he grew agitated. He went on:

'You're just making wild accusations, trying to get me to admit to who knows what. Well, then, if I'm not John Peterson, who am I?' He gave a triumphant laugh. 'Answer me that! You can't, can you? Because you've invented this whole story.'

'I know perfectly well who you are,' she replied. 'Your name is Jesse McKirdy, and according to all the newspapers you were murdered in your room at the Savoy Hotel in London on the 20th of May.'

That shocked him out of his complacency. He stared, astounded.

'How—'

'How did I know? An educated guess, let's say, and you've just confirmed it. Jesse McKirdy didn't die at the Savoy at all, did he? The man who died was the real John Billings Peterson, known to his friends as Bill. You killed him by hitting him on the head with the base of a heavy lamp, taking care to disfigure his face so nobody would recognize him. Then you left all your things with him, assumed his identity, took his luggage and set off to travel around Europe in his place. I don't know whether you resemble Bill at all, but Esther described him as being rather nondescript, so I assume you managed to get as far as Paris on Bill's passport, which is when you told me it got damaged—or you damaged it—and had to get a new one in a hurry, with your own picture on it. Did someone remark on Bill's photograph and cause you to lose your nerve?'

He did not reply. She went on:

'At any rate, you went to Paris and Rome and Athens in Bill's stead—took his holiday, in fact, using the tickets he'd already bought, one of which brought you to Rhodes the day before Edgar and I arrived. You had all the correct documents, and no-one had any reason to believe you were not who you said you were: John Billings Peterson, the grandson of John Peterson the oil magnate and the head of the Peterson Oil Corporation.'

She paused and watched as the man calling himself Peterson absent-mindedly picked up a large stone from the ground and began to fidget with it.

'Now, this part is more like guess-work. You can tell me whether it's right or not. I assume you were acquainted with Bill and Roy back in the States, but when you arrived in Rhodes on the 15th of June you had no idea that Bill was meant to be meeting Roy here, so you got a tremendous shock when Roy came to the Grand Hotel and asked for Bill. Roy was the one person who could bring your charade to an end and expose you as a murderer. You knew you were in terrible danger, so you had to act fast, either to get away from Rhodes immediately, or to silence Roy forever. The second course was safer from your point of view—besides, when you've committed murder once it's easy to do it again.

'I don't know exactly what went on between you, but somehow you managed to put him off. Then he told you he'd forgotten his passport, so you saw your chance and agreed to accompany him back to St. Michael in a taxi. Again, this is mostly guess-work, but for some reason you both got out of the taxi and went onto the cliff path. There you picked up a rock, hit Roy with it and shoved or dragged him over the edge of the cliff, then returned to Rhodes as though nothing had happened. I don't know where he'd left his suitcase, but you took it and kept it so as not to arouse suspicion.

'If you'd had any sense you'd have left the island the next day and nobody would have been any the wiser, but you couldn't resist coming to St. Michael to see the result of your little adventure. If Roy's body hadn't washed up I imagine you'd have gone away after a day or two, but he most obligingly stranded himself on Archangel Beach, where you and Philip Halliday found him. You might have left the place after that since there was nothing to connect you with his death, but unfortunately for you I turned up and started nosing about, and you began to feel in danger again because I wasn't convinced Cavell's death had been an accident. That's when you had the bright idea of pretending to be an amateur detective: that way you had an excuse to follow me about wherever I went in order to find out what I knew, while at the same time trying to throw me off the scent.

'First of all you claimed the death was suicide prompted by Mrs. Delisi's rejection of Roy. But you could see I didn't believe it and was still inclined to snoop about, so when we were up at the dig you thought it couldn't do any harm to try and put me out of the way. It was purely a spur of the moment attempt, but if it had succeeded it might easily have passed as an accident.

'Even then I don't suppose you were in any real danger of exposure, but unfortunately for you Miss Brinkhurst had taken it upon herself to search through the trunk Cavell left behind, and found something—I don't know what—that told her you had a connection to his death. On Saturday night before the dance she button-holed you in the reading-room and tried to black-mail you, so you arranged to meet her later on the beach, where you strangled her, then joined us at the dance at the Grand Hotel. Miss Brinkhurst's death nearly ruined everything, because you couldn't pretend it was an accident or suicide, but when they arrested those two fishermen you thought you were in the clear—until it turned out they had alibis and had to be released. Then you started to worry again, because you were the last person to have been seen speaking to Miss Brinkhurst, and I came to you with my inconvenient questions about what she'd said, and so forth. So to put me off the scent again you told me you'd overheard her blackmailing somebody. Of course, you were really telling me about what had happened to you, but I was wrapped up in my theory that Dr. Schulz was the guilty party and was only too happy to believe your story—and add a little to it myself.

'I might have gone on believing it until we found Bill's letter and Dr. Schulz told me he'd taken Roy into Rhodes, which shifted the scene of the action away from St. Michael. Once I found out your name was Billings and remembered you'd stayed at the Grand Hotel, I started to put two and two together. In addition to everything else I'd found out, Philip Halliday mentioned that you'd been in London at the time of the Chelsea flower show, which began on the 20th of May, the same date as the murder at the Savoy. It seemed incredible, but I decided to test out my theory by setting a little trap. If you were the murderer then it stood to sense you might have kept Roy's suitcase, so I got Edgar to make sure we were sitting at the next table to you at dinner, then pretended I'd spoken to the police, who were going to search all the rooms for the case. That was nonsense, incidentally—I've had no more luck in getting the police to listen to me than you have—but I wanted to see if you'd try and get rid of the case before the police turned up. And so you did.' She smiled. 'I congratulate you, by the way. You really did fool me with your act, and muddied the waters very nicely.'

He had listened in silence as she talked, but now he spoke.

'Well, this is all very nice, but you've no proof of anything. As I said, I found this suitcase in Dr. Schulz's room and you'll never prove I didn't.'

'It doesn't matter,' she replied. 'I've telegraphed to a friend of mine who's a reporter in London, asking him to send me a photograph of the real John Billings Peterson. I expect he can find one in the files somewhere, since he's rather an important business-man. And it ought to be easy enough to find the taxi-driver who brought you both to St. Michael that night—'

She did not have time to finish because at that moment Peterson decided to spring, launching himself towards her like lightning, his hand raised, ready to strike with the rock he had been holding. But before he reached her he found himself brought to the ground and his right hand pinned up his back with a steely grip.

'Oh, no you don't,' said Edgar, as Peterson yelped with pain. 'Yannis, give me a hand, won't you?'

Between them they subdued Peterson, and Yannis, who had been lurking in the shadows with Edgar, tied his hands behind his back with a length of rope.

'Good catch,' said Angela approvingly. 'He didn't even see you coming. Now, let's see what's in this suitcase—anything or nothing.'

She rummaged through Roy Cavell's things and brought something out. It was an envelope containing a letter and a cutting from a newspaper. She glanced at the letter and read the cutting.

'What is it?' said Edgar.

'Someone sent Roy a photograph of him and Bill from

224

their college days that made the paper. Whoever wrote the story conveniently put their names under the picture. This is what Miss Brinkhurst found in Roy's trunk—proof that you weren't the real John Billings Peterson. You took it from her after you killed her.' She glanced at Peterson. 'He didn't look much like you, but you've the same shaped face, so I imagine the passport people didn't look too closely. But why did you do it? Why did you murder Bill in the first place?'

'It was all his own fault,' spat Peterson. 'Nobody ever took me seriously or thought I was clever enough. Well I showed them, didn't I?'

'Suppose you tell us about it,' said Angela.

Now that he had been caught out he was only too willing to talk.

'I never did have much luck,' he said. 'My family lost everything in the crash, and I lost my job and couldn't get another until a friend of my father's hired me to carry some important insurance documents to a customer of his in London. He as good as told me he thought I was fit for nothing and that he was only doing it to help out Pa, so I'd better get it right or I was finished. He told me to book myself into the Savoy to make a good impression, but only gave me the money for two nights. For the rest of the stay I'd have to go somewhere cheaper.

'It was just my luck that my document case was stolen the day I arrived in London. I wired Pa's friend and of course got fired on the spot. So there I was, stuck in London feeling sorry for myself in a hotel I couldn't afford, making up my mind to use my ticket home, when I happened to bump into Bill. I'd known him and Roy in college, although we didn't run in the same circles because they were rich and I was a nobody from Indiana who had to scrape to get an education. Bill was the son of old John

Peterson's daughter, which is why he was called Billings. I heard he took the name Peterson after college when his parents died and his grandfather adopted him as his heir. After old Peterson died Bill inherited the whole company and set himself up as the big oil-man, with more money than anybody could possibly spend. You could see straight-away he'd done better in life than I had, wearing the best tailoring and throwing around five-dollar tips like rice at a wedding. I could have eaten well on that kind of money.

'He was friendly enough, but pretty condescending, which put me out somewhat. I didn't rise to the bait though, because I thought he might be minded to give me a job if I sucked up to him a little. At any rate, he came to my room and suggested we go out to dinner, then he looked me up and down and said that I'd better change first, as he wouldn't want to be seen with me, dressed as I was, here in London, where all the high-society people would look down on us if we weren't wearing the right things. Well, I didn't have much of a wardrobe of fancy dinner-suits—not like he did—and told him so. He laughed and started poking through my things, and was mighty rude about them. Maybe my clothes were a little shabby, but I wasn't a rich man like he was, and it wasn't polite of him to make fun of me for it. I got riled and spoke my mind, and somehow the story came out about my losing the documents and having to slink back home with my tail between my legs. At that he laughed even more, and said I'd always been a chump.

'Then I guess I saw red. I don't remember much, just that one minute he was alive and the next he was there lying on the floor of my room, dead, and I'd done it. You might think I'd have panicked, but I didn't.' His face assumed a proud expression. 'In fact, I had the idea of turning myself into Bill about two minutes after I killed him. After all, what did I have to lose? I was tired of being poor and put upon and laughed at all the time. I could take his place and find out what it was like to be rich for a few days, or a few weeks, or a few months, until they caught me.

'I couldn't believe how easy it was. Nobody suspected a thing, apart from once in Paris—that's when I got the new passport—and I began to think I'd never be caught. I had letters of credit and enough money to keep me going for months, and all Bill's rail and boat tickets, so I set myself to enjoy a tour of Europe using his itinerary.

'But when I got to Rhodes Cavell ruined it all. I was standing just behind him in the Grand Hotel when he asked for Bill at the desk, so you can imagine the fright I got when I recognized him. I scooted out of the way fast, then followed him into the bar and kept an eye on him from a safe distance while he sat and got thoroughly soaked —I guess over Mrs. Delisi. I might have made a bolt for it, but I'd got to enjoying myself as John B. Peterson and didn't see why I should let Cavell ruin all my beautiful plans, so I started thinking about how to get rid of him.

'I went up to his table and acted surprised, and let him believe I was there by pure coincidence, and pretended to look around for Bill. It was easy enough to fool him after all the drink he'd taken. It suited me to have him a little incapable, so I encouraged him to drink more and all the while I was wondering how to kill him. I couldn't do the same with Roy as I'd done with Bill, so I decided to get him to a lonely place outside and do it there. As luck would have it, he found out he'd forgotten his passport. I said I'd go to St. Michael with him to get it, and went out to look for a taxi. That nearly did for me: when I got back into the lobby the first thing I saw was Roy at the desk, asking for Bill again. The man at the desk saw me and pointed me out, which gave me the fright of my life.

'Luckily it didn't take too much to convince him that there'd been a mistake. I hustled him into the taxi and said I'd explain everything on the way. But I didn't have to in the end: when we were almost at the Hotel Acropolis he suddenly felt sick and we had to stop the taxi to get some fresh air. I followed him out, and—well—you know the rest. It was too dark for anybody to see what I was doing, and besides, it only took a minute. Afterwards I went back to the taxi and told the driver Roy had decided to walk the rest of the way to the hotel. He didn't care, just so long as nobody made a mess of his car. Then we went back to Rhodes and I went to bed. It was very easy,' he finished.

They all gazed at him in silence. He appeared perfectly unconcerned about what he had done.

'You really ought to have left the island while the going was good,' said Angela at last. 'I'd never have suspected a thing if you had. And you ought to have got rid of the suit-case too, as it's incriminating evidence. I don't know why you kept it.'

'It's a good suitcase, and the clothes are fine quality,' replied Peterson. 'I never had anything as fine as that back at home, and it's a sin to waste things.'

'It's a sin to commit murder, but that didn't seem to bother you,' observed Edgar. 'Oho, try that, will you?' he added, for with a sudden move Peterson had wrenched himself away from his captors and was making a bee-line for the cliff edge. With his hands tied behind him it was a futile effort, and he was soon subdued again.

'You won't get out of it that easily,' said Edgar. 'You've had your fun, now you'll face justice like a man.'

He gave Peterson a prod and the little party returned to the hotel in silence.

Chapter Twenty-Four

'I NEVER DID THINK he looked much like an oil-man,' said Angela next day at breakfast. 'And it was impossible to take him seriously as a detective, but it never occurred to me that it was all an act until I realized he was travelling under an alias. By then I knew he must be our murderer, but it was a bit of guess-work on my part about his being McKirdy, and I don't mind admitting I was holding my breath when I accused him of it. I'd have looked an awful idiot if I'd been wrong, but I didn't see how I could be. He was using Bill's name but thanks to Esther I knew he couldn't *be* Bill, so when I read that a man had been murdered at the Savoy at the same time as Bill was known to have stayed there, and that the body had been identified only by his luggage, I started to put two and two together and wonder whether it was Bill, rather than Jesse McKirdy, who had died in London. And if Jesse McKirdy, the supposed victim, was in fact still alive, it was obvious, firstly that he must have murdered Bill and taken his name, and secondly that Roy would have been a danger to him if they met. I knew the fake Peterson had been in London at the right time, and he talked of visiting the same places Bill mentioned in his letter, so it all seemed to fit. Incidentally, I did occasionally wonder why he wore such ill-fitting clothes, since he was meant to be so rich, but of course they weren't his.'

A reply had arrived from Freddy, who had telegraphed at length (on the *Clarion*'s money) to confirm what they had deduced—that the dead man was not Jesse McKirdy at all, but John Billings Peterson. It appeared that Scotland Yard had never been convinced the dead man was McKirdy, but had not yet been able to discover his real identity. In addition, Yannis had found the taxi-driver who had taken the fake Peterson and Roy Cavell from Rhodes to St. Michael that night. As Peterson had admitted, the two men had got out of the taxi shortly before they reached the Hotel Acropolis and instructed the driver to wait, but only one of them had returned, telling the driver his companion had decided to walk the rest of the way. The driver had had no reason to suspect anything, and had taken his passenger back to Rhodes then forgotten about it.

'McKirdy did a good job of fooling everyone,' replied Edgar. 'He might have looked harmless enough but I'd say he's one of the most dangerous men I've ever met—and I've met a few—given his propensity to commit murder at the least provocation.'

'He was tremendously conceited too,' said Angela. 'He really ought to have made his escape as quickly as possible after he killed Roy, but he couldn't resist coming to St. Michael to see the result of his crime. He was sure he wouldn't be caught, and he was very nearly right—he played the part of a comical little tourist so well that I almost didn't see through it. In fact, I rather wonder whether he hadn't convinced himself he *was* Peterson. He certainly took to his new identity easily enough, and seemed to believe the life of a rich man was nothing more than his due. I shouldn't be surprised if there were something of the fantasist about him.'

'Well, mad or bad, I wasn't about to give him the opportunity to have another go at you. I took good care to keep a close eye on you both while you were up there on the cliff top, just in case he decided to do something unpredictable.'

'Yes—even though I was careful to stand well away from him I was still slightly worried he might pounce at any moment. It was a toss-up as to whether he'd go for me or try to fling the suitcase off the cliff first, but he evidently decided I took precedence. After all, once I was dead he could get rid of the suitcase at his leisure.'

'At any rate, that was well played on your part. You put the wind up him nicely in the dining-room, then got him to admit to everything, which will save the police some effort. You weren't frightened out there, were you?'

She considered.

'No, I shouldn't say so. After all, you and Yannis were waiting close by and I knew you wouldn't let me come to any harm. As a matter of fact, I think I rather enjoyed it.'

He gave her a triumphant look.

'Exactly as I said—you'd rather have an adventure than not. You *like* the excitement, don't you?'

'That's not true at all!' She paused. 'Well, perhaps I do, just a little,' she admitted.

The news of Mr. Peterson's arrest had set the Hotel Acropolis into a great commotion, and everyone wanted to ask questions of Mr. and Mrs. Merivale, who it seemed had been responsible for bringing a dangerous murderer to justice. Their chances of a quiet honeymoon had never been great ever since Roy Cavell had turned up in the swimming-pool, but now it looked as though it would be quite impossible to get time to themselves, and so they began to think of returning to America. Edgar wanted to see to his horses, which had been sadly neglected, and since it had been two weeks since their unintended flight from Paris, they judged they ought to be safe from the loathsome Penn Piper, who was presumably in New York by now.

'We'll see to the tickets after breakfast,' said Edgar, although he did not seem in any hurry to move from his seat on the terrace, for the sunlight was dancing on the sea and the water was dotted with boats that scudded to and fro, and altogether it was easy to forget about the cares of ordinary life. Still, they could not stay here forever. Angela had a daughter to attend to, and there was still the tricky question of how Barbara and Edgar would get along, given the complicated circumstances surrounding Angela's marriage to him.

Her thoughts were interrupted by the arrival of Lady Trenoweth, who was being wheeled onto the terrace by Esther Grayson.

'Do you need the rug this morning?' said Esther. 'I know it's warm but there's a bit of a breeze and we don't want you to catch a chill, do we?'

'That is very kind of you, my dear, but it won't be necessary,' replied the old woman.

Something that might have been a smile spread across her face, and she looked most unlike herself. Esther settled her charge at the next table, then turned and caught sight of Angela and Edgar.

'I understand I have you to thank for finding out what happened to Roy.' A tear appeared in her eye and she dug in her pocket for a handkerchief. 'I'm sorry,' she said, as she dabbed at her eyes. 'I don't want you to think I'm ungrateful. The past few days have been hard, that's all.'

'I quite understand,' said Angela. 'And I'm sorry.'

'Don't be. I'm glad it's all come out into the open. I'd have hated going through life never knowing how or why he died.'

'You loved him very much, didn't you?'

'I did, but I've accepted now that it wouldn't have worked. It was the *idea* of being in love with him that had me so caught up, and I couldn't bear the thought that he didn't feel the same way about me as I did about him. If he hadn't died I guess I would have snapped out of it sooner or later. But I think I can let him go now.'

'Had you ever met Peterson—Jesse McKirdy—before?' asked Angela. 'He was at college with Roy, you know.'

'I met him once or twice in company, but I didn't know him to speak to. I did think he looked faintly familiar when he arrived here, but I didn't think too much about it.' Her face fell. 'I can't help thinking that if I'd recognized him earlier then poor Miss Brinkhurst might still be alive.'

Lady Trenoweth did not look as though she shared Esther's regret, but she made an effort.

'It's a pity, to be sure,' she said, 'but I am glad to have you instead.'

Angela regarded them both questioningly.

'Are you...'

Esther nodded.

'I've told Professor Delisi I don't want to work at the dig any more. To be perfectly honest, I was never really interested in archaeology and I only came here because of Roy. Rhodes has too many painful memories for me now, so it's time for me to leave.'

'Miss Grayson is going to come back to England with me and be my companion,' said Lady Trenoweth.

'Now, you know I can't promise to look after you forever,' said Esther good-humouredly. 'But I'll see you settled back at home and stay with you a while until you find someone who suits you better than Miss Brinkhurst did.'

She looked up as Philip Halliday just then joined them.

'Did you get your tickets?' she asked him. 'It's very kind of you to accompany us back.'

'Oh, you're going with them, are you?' asked Angela.

'Yes,' he replied. 'My publisher wants the book by October but there are too many distractions here and I'll never get it finished if I stay.'

Sophia Delisi swayed onto the terrace as he spoke, but he did not even see her, for he was looking at Esther.

'Do you think you'll finish it on time?' Angela wanted to know.

'I think so. I've got the first few chapters written now and I've some good ideas as to how the story ought to develop. I rather think it might be my best work yet.'

'Splendid,' said Angela. 'I look forward to reading it.'

Philip turned to Miss Grayson.

'What about the taxi to Rhodes? Did you manage to book it?'

She grimaced.

'I couldn't get a straight answer out of them. You'd think it would be an easy enough thing to arrange, wouldn't you?'

'That idiot Florakis—I don't know who put him in charge of running a hotel. I'll speak to him for you.'

Esther stood up and they disappeared indoors. Angela watched them go with a smile. She had the distinct impression that Sophia Delisi and Roy Cavell would soon be forgotten.

They finished breakfast and were preparing to leave when Lady Trenoweth cleared her throat and fixed them with a stern stare.

'I have been meaning to speak to the both of you about

something very disturbing that has come to my attention,' she announced. 'Before she came to her unfortunate end Amy Brinkhurst informed me that I have been sharing a hotel with two—*gaol-birds*, I believe they call it. What have you to say to that?'

Angela and Edgar exchanged glances.

'It's quite true,' replied Angela after a moment. 'But it's part of our past now and not something we care to put about publicly, so it's rather impolite of you to bring the subject up, if you don't mind my saying so. We've come for a holiday like anybody else and we've just as much right to be here as you have.'

'Hmph,' said Lady Trenoweth. 'You're a pert one. Did she try and extort money out of you when she found out? She was a blackmailer through and through.'

'Not exactly,' replied Angela. 'But I shouldn't have paid her a penny if she had.'

'Good. I'm glad to see you have some backbone at least. And I gather you have helped catch a dangerous murderer, so I suppose there's some good in you. Just make sure you keep out of trouble in future.'

She gave them a nod of dismissal.

'Not as difficult as you thought, was it?' said Edgar as they walked away.

'No,' she replied reflectively.

'Then perhaps this little experiment of ours will be a success. You did think of it as an experiment, didn't you?' he said slyly.

Since this was uncomfortably true, Angela did not reply. He laughed.

'Let's go and see to those tickets,' he said.

———

Sophia Delisi was sitting in the reading-room with her magazine when Angela came to return the newspapers she had taken the day before.

'So you have found the man who killed Roy,' she said. 'I am glad. But why did you not leave your husband to take care of it instead of going out with him in the middle of the night?'

'He did take care of it. He was the one who captured McKirdy, but I was the one who found him in the first place so I wasn't going to be left out of it at the finish,' Angela answered.

'How strange.' Sophia regarded Angela with her head on one side. 'They tell me you are a famous detective.'

'Not exactly.'

'You must be very clever. I could never do as you do, and find bad people just by asking them questions. What if you choose the wrong person?'

'I did choose the wrong person to start with,' replied Angela. 'More than one wrong person, in fact. If you'll believe it, I even suspected your husband for a while.'

'Aldo?' She seemed entertained. 'Why Aldo?'

'Because of you. Somebody said you—you'd been unlucky—' she had been going to say, 'were bad luck,' but caught herself just in time '—because you lost your first husband and at least two other men who wanted to marry you back in Salonika. So when Roy died I did wonder for a little while whether the professor mightn't have had something to do with it because he didn't like men getting too close to you and wanted you all to himself. I do apologize: of course it was an absurd idea.'

'It is not an absurd idea,' said Mrs. Delisi. 'I have often wondered the same thing myself.'

She said it in her usual matter-of-fact manner, and

seemed unconscious of the astonishment she had caused in her interlocutor.

'I beg your pardon?'

'It may be that I am wrong, of course. I have never asked him.'

Angela gaped.

'But shouldn't you like to know for certain?' she said weakly.

'Why should I? If it is true it would only cause trouble, and I do not want to cause trouble. I love Aldo.' She smiled. 'And besides, it is the job of every man to protect his wife, no?'

It was on the tip of Angela's tongue to say, 'Not to that extent,' but she could see that she and Mrs. Delisi thought very differently on the matter, so she did not. It explained Sophia's shocked reaction to the death of Roy Cavell, however: evidently her suspicions had immediately flown to her husband.

'Should you have minded if Aldo had been the one who killed Roy?' she could not help asking curiously.

'Yes,' replied Sophia. 'The others were all very bad, you see. But Roy was a good man. I did not want him to die.'

'I see,' said Angela. There seemed nothing more to be said, so she bade Sophia goodbye and turned to leave.

'I wish you a good journey,' said Mrs. Delisi, and turned back to her magazine.

———

THEY WENT to pay one last visit to Georgios, who wanted to know whether it was true that Dr. Schulz had been released pending further investigation into his activities, and had promptly made his escape from Rhodes. Angela and Edgar had no idea, but supposed the news would get around soon enough if it were true. Kostis would be sure to tell them, at least.

'Poor Professor Delisi,' said Edgar as they returned to the hotel. 'He seems to be losing archaeologists at a tremendous rate. First Cavell, then Schulz and Miss Grayson. There'll be nobody left soon.'

Angela expressed her agreement, but privately she thought that it was safer all round to avoid working for the professor if possible. Schulz had never shown any particular interest in Sophia Delisi, but who knew how little it took for the professor's suspicions to be aroused with regard to his wife? Perhaps Schulz's escape had been luckier than he knew.

At last their luggage was packed and they were ready to leave for Rhodes, and the ferry to the mainland. As Angela waited for Edgar to speak to Yannis about the taxi she saw Lady Trenoweth enter the lobby, leaning heavily on her stick. The old woman nodded distantly to her. Angela hesitated for a second, then made up her mind and approached her.

'Why did you say, "Cheated at the last," when Miss Brinkhurst died?' she asked without preamble.

Lady Trenoweth regarded her frostily.

'That is none of your business,' she replied.

'It isn't, but fair exchange is no robbery and you know my secret now, so won't you tell me yours?' said Angela boldly.

'Hmph. You *are* a pert one, aren't you? Let us say I was denied satisfaction, that's all.'

'From Miss Brinkhurst?'

Lady Trenoweth said nothing, and Angela suddenly understood.

'She was blackmailing you too, wasn't she? What did she have on you?'

'You needn't bother asking, because I have no intention of telling you,' snapped the old lady. A look of deep irritation passed across her face, then she burst out, '*Five years* I was forced to put up with that odious woman, for naturally I could not get rid of her once she told me what she knew to my disadvantage.'

'Poor you,' said Angela sympathetically.

'She forced me to make a will in her favour, and I dared not refuse for fear of what she would do if I did. You might say I ought to have stood up to her, but I am a frail old woman and I did not.' A smile played about her lips. 'But I had planned my revenge. She used to taunt me with the will, but she did not know about the second will I had made at a later date, which would have superseded it, and which left all the money to a cats' home. I have no particular love of cats, but Amy Brinkhurst disliked them intensely, and on the worst days I gained no little amount of pleasure from the thought of her face when she found out I had bested her. But after what has happened I no longer have that pleasure.' She directed an ironic look at Angela. 'Still, she is dead and I am alive, so I suppose I have won.'

'I suppose you have,' said Angela.

She watched as the old woman went slowly into the dining-room, then turned to look for Edgar, who was directing the loading of their luggage into the taxi. She had said all her goodbyes, so there was just time for one last glance through the terrace doors at the view of the sea. It had been an eventful honeymoon to say the least, and she was ready to go home, but she would be sorry to leave Rhodes. Perhaps she would return one day. She turned away and went to hand the keys in at the desk and say goodbye to Mr. Florakis, then Edgar came to join her.

'All ready?' he said with a smile.

She smiled back.

'All ready.'

'Then let's go,' he said.

———

New Releases

If you'd like to receive news of further releases by Clara Benson, you can sign up to my mailing list here: clarabenson.com/newsletter.

Books by Clara Benson

THE ANGELA MARCHMONT MYSTERIES

THE FREDDY PILKINGTON-SOAMES ADVENTURES

SHORT STORIES

Angela's Christmas Adventure

The Man on the Train

A Question of Hats

COLLECTIONS

Angela Marchmont Mysteries Books 1-3

Angela Marchmont Mysteries Books 4-6

Freddy Pilkington-Soames Adventures Books 1-3

HISTORICAL FICTION

In Darkness, Look for Stars (published by Bookouture)

The Stolen Letter (published by Bookouture)

OTHER

The Lucases of Lucas Lodge

Made in the USA
Las Vegas, NV
14 June 2023